W9-CEC-120

The Gallery

The Gallery

LAURA·MARX·FITZGERALD

Dial Books for Young Readers

Dial Books for Young Readers
Penguin Young Readers Group
An imprint of Penguin Random House LLC
375 Hudson Street, New York, NY 10014

Copyright © 2016 by Laura Marx Fitzgerald

Library of Congress Cataloging-in-Publication Data
Names: Fitzgerald, Laura Marx, author.
Title: The gallery / Laura Marx Fitzgerald.
Description: New York, NY : Dial Books for Young Readers, [2016] |
Summary: In 1929 New York City, twelve-year-old housemaid Martha O'Doyle suspects
that a wealthy recluse may be trying to communicate with the outside world
through the paintings on her gallery walls.
Identifiers: LCCN 2015029009 | ISBN 9780525428657 (hardback)
Subjects: | CYAC: Mystery and detective stories. | Household
employees—Fiction. | Art—Fiction. | Irish Americans—Fiction. | New York
(N.Y.)—History—1898–1951—Fiction. | BISAC: JUVENILE FICTION / Mysteries
& Detective Stories. | JUVENILE FICTION / Historical / United States /
20th Century. | JUVENILE FICTION / Art & Architecture.
Classification: LCC PZ7.F575357 Gal 2016 | DDC [Fic]—dc23
LC record available at http://lccn.loc.gov/2015029009

Printed in the United States of America

1 3 5 7 9 10 8 6 4 2

Design by Jennifer Kelly
Text set in New Baskerville ITC Pro

For Mom and Dad
and
Anne Cope

The Gallery

Chapter 1
May 2016

One of the tabloid papers, the *New York Yodel*, has a midsection where they feature some poor sap who's hung around long enough to make it to one hundred.

This time, the poor sap is me.

Last week the paper sent this young whip of a girl to interview me. She bounced around the linoleum room, poking around the photos on my bureau.

"Is she awake?" she asked Jolene, the day nurse, like I wasn't even there, and as soon as I stirred, she started shouting questions like "What's the secret to happiness?" in my ear.

Like living to one hundred makes you happy, and not creaky and constipated.

I just gave the addled smile I use to make people

think I'm senile and pointed lamely to my throat. I haven't been able to speak for thirty years, since I had my voice box removed. Cancer of the larynx. Don't smoke, kids.

"Oh, right," the young reporter ducked her head. "I forgot. Well, here—" she thrust a legal pad and a pen into my lap. "You can write the answers."

I held up my gnarled hands and shrugged. Arthritis.

"Oh." She gingerly picked up the pad and pen again, afraid to brush against my paper-thin skin. Back they went into this large satchel like newsboys used to carry. "Do you know," she said, rustling around for something else, "I looked you up in our archives, and I found you! Martha O'Doyle, right? I checked the dates. This must be you." She pulled out a regular sheet of paper, but printed on it was an old newspaper article. It was the last time I was in the papers, eighty-seven years ago. I recognized the headline.

March 26, 1929

BOMB KILLS NEWSPAPER TYCOON AND HIS "WILD ROSE"!

———

Priceless Art Collection Destroyed!

———

Rose "battier than a church bell!" says maid.

———

2

New York society was rocked last night by a bomb that exploded just past midnight in the home of newspaper tycoon, J. Archer Sewell. Killed in the blast were both Mr. Sewell and his wife, the former Rose Pritchard, heiress to the Union-Eastern Railroad fortune.

The couple's lavish Fifth Avenue mansion, once site of some of society's most opulent entertainments, was destroyed.

Lost, too, was Mrs. Sewell's art collection, described as "unrivaled" by experts and glimpsed only by guests of the increasingly reclusive Sewell family. The collection—which included paintings by great artists like Rembrandt, Caravaggio, Courbet, as well as living painters like the "modern" sensation, Pablo Picasso—was speculated to be worth millions.

As of this morning, it is an ash heap.

The attack came as no surprise to J. Archer Sewell's detractors. As publisher of this newspaper's rival, the *Daily Standard*, Sewell was known as a staunch defender of traditional American values in today's rocky times. His hard-charging rhetoric made him not a few enemies, especially among immigrants, "wets," anarchists, and other targets of his paper's wrath.

Yet the drawing rooms of Fifth Avenue are abuzz that "Wild Rose" herself may have been behind the bombing. The former Miss Pritchard's outrageous teen-aged antics are familiar to the *Yodel*'s more faithful readers. The young heiress was rumored to have suffered a mental breakdown shortly after her marriage.

Sources close to the heiress say that her behavior had become increasingly erratic, and in recent years she often refused to leave her rooms. Mrs. Sewell's more recent outbursts were captured in this very paper.

But was this former debutante capable of an act of such shocking violence?

"I wouldn't put it past her," shared Martha O'Doyle, a young housemaid of Irish extraction. "She was nuttier than a fruit cake, always howling in her room like a right lunatic. If you ask me, she set off that bomb herself.

"She should've been locked up in a madhouse," continued the outspoken young "colleen." "It was only through Mr. Sewell's kindness, God bless him, that she could remain in her home, with all her comforts about her." Here young Martha stopped to wipe her eyes. "He was a true gentleman, Mr. Sewell was."

However, detectives are investigating all possible suspects, including members of the Sewell household staff, one of whom is said to have recently fled the country. Police were unable to share more details, but have asked readers to come forward with any information that might aid their investigation.

I let the page flutter to my lap.

Like most stories in the paper, it was full of lies.

"I've been reading up on the bombing. Did you know you're the only living eyewitness?" the girl reporter said breathlessly, her pen at the ready. "The only one who knows what really happened."

I shrugged again.

She heaved a frustrated sigh, her schemes to move off the back page human-interest stories clearly roadblocked. "I mean, you're a hundred years old! You won't last forev—"

Here I pretended to fall asleep, which I sometimes do in the middle of conversations anyway. By the way she poked my arm with her finger, I could tell she thought I had joined the heavenly choir. When I heard her footsteps die away, I opened my eyes again. Her business card was resting on my lap.

═══

Today, a week later, the morning staff crowded around my bed singing *Happy Birthday*, and Jolene brought me the paper.

"Now, looka you, Miz O'Doyle. You just as pretty as evah," she said as she opened it up to my photo.

LOCAL LASS LICKS 100!

Miss Martha O'Doyle, lifelong Brooklyn resident and longtime bon vivant, raises a glass of bubbly to celebrate her hundredth! She credits her astonishing longevity to "always looking on the bright side."

I didn't say any of that. The picture shows me sitting in my wheelchair with a glass of champagne the girl reporter stuck in my hand; I didn't drink that either. All I can take are these energy shakes now.

"And whatta nice smile," continued Jolene. "Like a beauty queen."

I was just trying to stifle a belch. Which was nice of me, I thought, because usually I don't bother. I gave the paper back to Jolene and had her wheel me over to the window.

Most folks at Shaded Acres (actually a sun-blasted high-rise surrounded by "acres" of Brooklyn concrete) won't take rooms on the cemetery side. But I requested this side for the same reason I always ride in the front seat: I like to see where I'm going.

I can see where I've been, too. Because from my window, I can make out Rose's final resting place on the hill. Even though it's surrounded by auto-body shops today, Green-Wood Cemetery was once the final destination of the rich and fancy, and lucky for me those folks paid their gardeners in perpetuity.

At this time of year, I have front-row seats to the spectacle. First the shock of yellow forsythia against the bleak gray sky, then the Japanese magnolias, the cherry blossoms, the lilacs. After the grand finale—the climbing roses—the summer leaves fill in like a curtain coming down on a show. And I have to wait until winter strips the place bare before I catch sight of the Pritchard family plot again.

Every spring, it's like Rose is signaling me in this blooming-and-dying Morse code: Meet me here.

That girl reporter was right. This would likely be my last spring show, my last message from Rose, my last chance to tell my story.

The next day, I got one of those youngster volunteers to show me how the computers work. He brought me the kind that folds up and showed me how to open a page, type on it, erase my mistakes.

The day after that, I rubbed some Ben-Gay into my hands, gave up my Jell-O to Saint Peter for a little more longevity, and, with my crooked fingers, I looked for the truth among the keys.

Chapter

2

September 1928

I learned early that if you ask an adult for the truth, usually you get a story.

Sometimes two.

Take the story of my birth. My dad said that Ma labored brave and hard all night with me all topsy-turvy in her belly—never leading with my head, sure, nothing's changed, he'd say—and that as I finally made my way into the world, the dawn broke and light streamed in through the window, sunbeams warming up both sets of cheeks. And the doctor said I was the most beautiful baby he'd ever delivered, and I should be named Aurora for the goddess of the dawn, and Daddo still wishes that's what they'd named me.

My ma said that's malarkey, that I was born in

the unnaturally hot blaze of a May afternoon, with a single nurse and not a doctor to be found for the likes of a poor mick like her, and how would Daddo know anything about it when he was at the saloon the whole time? And my name was always going to be Martha, for my great-aunt Martha who paid my ma's passage over from Ireland when she was a girl.

Which one is true? Maybe both, probably neither.

So this time, I'm telling the story.

I mean, the truth.

Late September in Brooklyn can be delightful, with wisps of fall in the air, or it can be as hot and muggy as August.

That was the kind of day it was when I sat in catechism class, trying not to let Sister Ignatius see me scratching my sweaty behind under my regulation wool tights. I had an idea that I might sneak out and walk to the elevated train. I'd be at Coney Island before French class even started, to *la diablo* with Mademoiselle Flanagan.

I figured I could fake lady complaints and ask for a pass to the nurse. Flanagan would think I was at the nurse's office, and the other girls would tell our last period calisthenics teacher I was excused from exercises. As a plan, it couldn't fail.

"Martha O'Doyle, I asked you a question."

"May I go to the nurse, Sister?" I doubled over my desk. "It's my time."

"Well, how apropos, as we were just talking about the Curse of Eve. And wasn't it the curse last week when I asked you to recite the Second Lesson on God and His Perfections? And the week before that when it was your turn to clap the erasers?"

I groaned louder and clutched my stomach.

"Or could this be your punishment for ignoring your studies last night?"

I'd meant to memorize the Fifth Lesson after I fed, bathed, and tucked my little brothers into their prayed-over bedsides. But I'd heard on the way home that Declan Leary bet Jimmy Ratchett that he could pull his dad's Ford around the block with his teeth. (He couldn't.) So after the show, the boys and I wheedled beer-splashed peanuts off of Dom Donovan's speakeasy and hosed off under a fire hydrant. By the time Ma got home from her job in Manhattan, all she saw was a clean kitchen and wet heads on the pillow.

So, no, there'd been no time to weigh the sins of Eve.

"So I will ask you again, Miss O'Doyle: How was Eve tempted to sin? Speak from personal experience if you can't remember the details."

The other girls giggled, damn them.

"Erm . . . a snake. No, a serpent."

"Yes, Eve was tempted into sin by the Devil, who came in the form of a snake and persuaded her to break God's command. And that command was?"

"To eat . . . I mean, not to eat the apple."

"The fruit of the Tree of Knowledge. And which were the chief causes that led Eve into sin?"

Now my stomach really did churn. Before bed I'd flicked through an issue of *Dime Detective*, not the Bible. So I casted around for words left over from Father Quinlan's homilies. Fruit. Sin. Naked. Shame. Knowledge.

"Knowledge."

"What about knowledge?"

"She—Eve—wanted to know. To know what God knew. What he forbade her from knowing."

"Yes, this was the primary sin: She admired what was forbidden instead of shunning it. And the other—"

"Hold a tick," I heard myself saying.

"What did you just say, Miss O'Doyle?"

"I mean, just a minute. Why was Eve punished for knowledge? Ain't—sorry, Sister—isn't that what we're all sent here to do? Learn things?"

"Just like our spiritual parents, Adam and Eve,

you are here to learn the things God deemed fit and right to learn."

"And how are you supposed to know that something's not fit and right until you, well, know it already? That's a bit of a barn door behind the horse. It just seems to me Eve got a bum rap is all. Whoever wrote this thing—"

"This thing! Is that how you refer to the living Word of Our Lord?"

"The Bible, I mean. Whoever wrote it sort of put it all on Eve. Who can blame her for wanting to know some big secret like that? And why does God point it out so much and then forbid it? I know that if Ma tells my little brothers, 'Don't go eating the pie I just made,' I'll find their fingers in it as soon as her back is turned. Better to just hide it under the bed and let them wonder why the place smells of cherries."

"Martha Doyle, I warn you to stop talking this instant."

Here's the thing. Once I set to wondering something, my mind skips straight ahead. Like my brothers running into traffic.

"And I don't see how Adam is some great hero in this story. It's not like he took too much convincing to do the same thing Eve had the guts to do first.

Why'd Eve get the curse? Why can't boys spend a week out of every month sitting on a rag bundle like the rest of us?"

As I paused to contemplate Declan Leary and his gang complaining of cramps, I caught sight of Sister Ignatius's face. It resembled a mushroom I once saw at a Chinatown market: squat, purple, and bloated.

And I knew that, just like Eve, my wonderings had gotten me expelled from what would—in retrospect—seem like Paradise.

"You think your schooling is some grand joke? Well, missy, you're about to get a taste of the life of labor. You'll see what I've been warning you about."

My ma's nasal Irish tones carried over the clacking of the elevated train. She lectured her way over the Manhattan Bridge, but I let my attention wander out the train window, to the boats in the harbor, lit up by the early morning sun, and Lady Liberty waving us over to the Manhattan side.

"Sit down properly, and stop your gawking out the window. Dear me." Ma shifted her address to the more general public as she waved away a gust of dust. A gentleman next to us rushed to close her window. Ma had that effect on people. She gave him a nod and resettled her hat. "I've arranged a position under Mon-soor Lerblanc, the cook. Lucky you we binned a kitchen maid this week. Let's see how a year washing pots and chopping onions compares to a bit of study."

Sister Ignatius had told my mother enough was enough, probably with some Latin thrown in, and that I was a bad influence on my fellow pupils at the Blessed Name of Our Holy Mother parish school. Ma, no less formidable a force, was able to negotiate my expulsion down to a year's withdrawal, with a conditional seat the following fall, assuming I'd learned my lesson.

What lesson, my mother was happy to spell out in vivid detail. My school uniform was handed in, and the evening care and keeping of the twins was entrusted to our downstairs lodger, Mrs. Annunziata, for a reduction in rent and all the cheeks she could pinch. I would be going to work with my mother at the Fifth Avenue mansion where she was the head housekeeper.

My ma's job was a good one, all said. She'd gone to work there when my dad returned to the road. Daddo was a vaudeville star, performing his act around the country, selling out houses to the rafters. But due to shifty bookers and managers, he was always chasing his pay, and it fell on Ma to make ends meet.

With her extra wages, my ma had managed to get us a tidy house in Brooklyn with room for a lodger. And ever since the mansion's butler left, my ma had been in charge of the whole staff, even the footmen, which was quite the accomplishment back then. But as her employer said, "Why not? It's running a house, not running for president."

Her employer was Mr. J. Archer Sewell, a big-shot type who owned a newspaper. My mother's face always lit up when she described him to me.

"A true gentleman, Mr. Sewell is. Generous not just to me, but to all the staff. At Christmas, all the housemaids were given hair combs with real crystals, and the footmen got silk suspenders. And a ham. All paid for out of Mr. Sewell's pocket."

I couldn't imagine some ham and fripperies made much of a dent in a millionaire's pocket, but Ma had momentarily forgotten my shortcomings, so I held my tongue.

"How lucky that you were born in America! Back when I worked at a grand house in Ireland, the maids were expected to turn their faces to the wall when the employer walked by! There's a fine how-de-do. But not Mr. Sewell. We're all 'part of the team,' he says, from the lowest scullery maid all the way up to the top." She smiled; the *top* was her.

"Sounds like quite a large staff for a bachelor. What's he need all those maids for?"

Ma sniffed. "One of the largest houses on the avenue requires a full staff, and as it is, we are quite short-handed. Just two housemaids to clean a ball-room, dining room, art gallery, not to mention all the bedrooms. And a footman with nothing to do but open the door now and then." She tsked her tongue, for Ma hated nothing more than idleness.

I was just about to ask after my duties in the kitchen when she spoke again. "He's not a bachelor, exactly."

"Who?"

"Mr. Sewell, of course. He has a wife. Quite ill, though."

"What's wrong with her? She got gout?" That was the only rich people's disease I could think of.

"Nothing with her body. It's her mind. She's . . ."

"A loony?"

Ma looked down her nose at me. "An invalid. A nervous type. She has strange fears and reactions to things. She doesn't leave her rooms."

"What, ever?"

"In a few years, I believe."

"A few *years*!"

"Shhhhhh!" Ma's eyes darted around the train

car, but the commuters were mostly snoring or absorbed in the morning headlines. "The most important thing a servant brings to a job is—"

"I know, the apron." I held mine up. "I went back for it, remember?"

"You must do something about this habit of interrupting. I was going to say: discretion. Mr. Sewell depends on us to attend to Mrs. Sewell, to keep her calm and comfortable, and above all to keep her out of trouble. And the papers, for that matter."

"I don't see how anyone could make the papers if they never leave the house."

Ma chuckled. Chuckled, mind you. At home she was tired and irritable, put out over an upset water jug or the twins' boots in the doorway. But when she talked about this other house, this other family, she was—well, different. Assured. Animated. Even happy.

"Miss Rose—I mean, Mrs. Sewell—used to be quite the scandal maker. I remember one time—"

"Hold the phone, did you know her then?"

"You may say 'I beg your pardon,' and before I rose to housekeeper, I was her lady's maid, back when she was Rose Pritchard. Miss Rose was what they call 'new money,' or her father was, at least. A fortune dug out of the West Virginia coal mines and built into a railroad. Mr. Pritchard used that money to move to New York, buy their place in society: all the best schools, the big house, the right parties. Every privilege in the world, and Rose didn't give two figs for any of it. She was always looking for trouble—and finding it, I might add." And Ma chuckled that chuckle again.

"This Rose sounds like a spoiled brat," I mumbled.

I thought Ma would jump to her charge's defense, but instead she seemed to weigh my comment. "She was, somewhat. They were the sort of shenanigans you'd see from the girls on the lane, sneaking out to nightclubs and such. But it was more than that. It was like she was trying to prove something to her father. There he'd gone to all that time and money to give her the place in society he'd never had. But all she wanted was to prove she could make herself from nothing, like him.

"Like the time she told us she was doing charity work at one of the settlements downtown, when really she was working in a sweatshop, learning to sew neckties. 'Learning the business from the ground up,' she said, before her father put a stop to it. Then she ran off to Paris, living with unsavory types, buying their pictures; she swore they were worth something. And oh!" Ma laughed again. "The capers! Like the time she dressed like a gypsy woman and stood outside begging money off her father's dinner guests. By the time dessert had been cleared, she burst in, claiming she'd turned the money three times over at the track. This, at a time when her father's company was failing its investors. Oh, Mr. Pritchard was furious!"

"So, what happened?"

"What happens to most girls, same as me. She got married. She settled, eventually. And then—"

Her smile faded, and her face sank back into the lines I knew so well. "It all seemed harmless, back then."

Then the train went dark, plunging underground as we reached the Manhattan side of the river.

Chapter 3

In all the years my mother talked about working at "the house," I'm not sure what I pictured. Probably a house, and not a castle flown in from a fairy story. Its spires and turrets were visible all the way from Park Avenue, and as we turned onto Fifth, I could see that nearly half the block was taken up with marble and stone and stained-glass windows that put our parish church to shame. It faced Central Park, just across the avenue, and mimicked it with a lushly landscaped walkway that guided you up to a door like a drawbridge.

But the grotesque stone lions on either side, claws at the ready, functioned as gatekeepers to the likes of me and Ma. We traveled round to a side street and down a dark set of stairs that took us to the servants' entrance. All the working rooms of the house—practically a house in a house, with the kitchen, laundry, pantries, and even the servants' hall where we'd eat meals—were underground, echoing with the clattering of brooms and pans and rumbling every time a subway train ran by. This parallel underworld was where I'd be toiling under the supervision of Monsieur Leblanc, the famed chef snatched up from Paris and brought to New York as Mr. Sewell's personal cook.

But before I could be plunged into my new life as a kitchen maid, Ma wanted to show off the fruits of her labor. I was just as eager to see that famed "house" that drew Ma out of bed at dawn and didn't let her go till she'd fussed and fixed its ornaments like a spoiled and demanding mistress. So with my apron now pressed and doffed and Ma's spit holding down my hair, I was allowed a tour.

Maybe it was the imported white marble, which dominated from floor to stairs to ceiling, or maybe it was the way Ma's words of pride bounced from one room to the next, but the house gave me shivers. The front rooms were quite spectacular, with pianos of gold and sofas of satin and so many shiny things a magpie would fly itself into a tizzy. But the deeper you went, the more rooms were closed up, curtains drawn so as not to disturb the furniture, which hibernated under protective drapes. I couldn't tell if the rooms were simply unused, or if the rooms' contents had been deemed so valuable that the owners' could not risk accidental human contact.

Even the house's centerpiece, the glass-ceilinged courtyard with its show-offy, mismatched jumble of orchids, lilacs, and orange trees, seemed false to me, a place where plants were forced to flourish no matter the season or their God-given instructions.

But most unsettling were the walls. No matter where you went, no matter how opulent the furnishings, every room was haunted by ghosts: a chessboard of discolored squares and rectangles on the silk wallpaper, nails left behind like you'd see in a cheap boardinghouse.

"Where are all the pictures?" I asked Ma in a whisper. It only seemed right to whisper. "Stolen?"

Ma seemed annoyed. "Not exactly. Miss Rose—that's Mrs. Sewell to you, by the way—she keeps them in her rooms." She paused. "They comfort her."

In the glare of all things golden, I'd almost forgotten about the house's resident lunatic. I pricked up my ears, listening for the distant howls of a madwoman. But there was nothing but the same silence, from room to entombed room.

I was never so happy to hear it was time to go to work.

An hour later I was elbows up in scalding water, sweat pouring down in streams, scrubbing the remains of some food charred past recognition off the bottom of a pot. My introduction to Chef (as he insisted I call him) consisted of a grunt and the splash of a hot pan tossed into a greasy sink. And another. And another. It became quickly apparent that Chef had had a whole kitchen of assistants and sub-assistants and dishwashers and sub-dishwashers in Paris, and not just one girl who usually told her mother she made her brothers a nice, home-cooked meal but really bought them dinner at the frankfurter cart.

By the end of a week, I'd learned to do the work of at least ten French boys. I chopped onions, ground garlic, boned chicken, and rendered lard. When I wasn't cooking, I was washing dishes; when I wasn't washing, I was drying; and when I wasn't doing either, I was learning French under Chef's instruction. *Brunoise* meant he wanted "things cut into little cubes," *bâtonette* meant "little sticks," and *idiote* meant just what you'd think it did.

Mademoiselle Flanagan's French class, with its

bright, sunny classroom where I could doodle and play pranks when the work didn't suit me, seemed like an exotic paradise, lunch and recess like a luxury. Now I ate lunch alone every day. I'd hustle to get the noon dinner on the table for the other servants—Ma, plus her two housemaids, Bridie and Magdalena, and the footman, Alphonse—who filed into the servants' hall without a glance my way. I supposed they, like their employers, assumed the food was the result of some subterranean magic. And the cleaning, too; I toiled alone over the pots while Chef smoked a cigarette in the alley and a quiet murmur of polite conversation drifted out of the lunchroom. Once Ma's team had returned above stairs, I'd clean up their dishes and eat leftovers at the sink. Over my head, by the street level window, I'd watch a parade of feet carry their owners to destinations with conversation, laughter, and sunlight.

My mind kept going back to the time we went to the Rockaways, when I sat all day on the pier, unable to swim and unwilling to learn. As the sun went down, Daddo claimed he saw a puppy in the water, and when I leaned over to get a better look, I felt his foot on my backside. Next thing I knew, I was at the bottom of the ocean, sunk like a stone.

I screamed, but with the air replaced by water around me, no sound came out. I looked up to the sky and saw light streaming, white water, legs thrashing with wild abandon, but heard only a muted, distant fog. Terrified, I flailed and kicked until I broke through to the surface, desperate to leave that watery universe behind.

That's what working below stairs was like, I realized too late—like living underwater. There was a world up there, above the surface, brighter and shinier than this one, divined only in glimpses and muffled echoes.

For example, there were Mr. Sewell's food requests. These seemingly random menus, summoned from on high, were all we saw of a revolving calendar of late-night suppers, always held after most of the servants had left for the night, always contrived for a guest list of one. Their identities, a mystery to all but the footman who served them, clearly dictated the cuisine. One night it was herring and pickles. Another night it was a six-course meal of Neapolitan splendors. Another was nothing but oysters. Each request set off scavenger hunts through the well-stocked pantry—a floor-to-ceiling emporium that rattled and shuddered whenever a subway train ran nearby.

Sometimes the word came down that Mr. Sewell would be dining out after all, and the vegetables Chef had spent all day carving into flower shapes were thrown angrily into the bin.

Then there were the particular culinary needs of Mrs. Sewell, and these I studied most closely for clues to the madness. The mysterious lady partook of the same uninspired menu, day in day out. In the mornings, there was toast and tea, with some broth or boiled vegetables for lunch. And in the early evening, just a bowl of porridge.

Any chink in this feast of blandness could spark some kind of fit. So the toast had to be golden, with nary a burnt spot, and the water for the tea had to be caught before it rolled over to a boil. And the porridge must have some fancy sugar stirred into it that Mr. Sewell secured from some specialty grocer and which was kept in a big jar next to the tea things.

Because the sight of anyone at mealtime made Mrs. Sewell *overstimulated*, the tray had to be loaded into the dumbwaiter, a sort of cupboard-sized miniature elevator that traveled up from the kitchen, past the dining room, past the second floor hallway, all the way up to a turret at the tippy-top of the house, directly into her suite of rooms. She'd nibble her meal in that protected solitude, then send the plates back down in the dumbwaiter to be washed (by me).

This was what it meant to be rich, I'd think as I hoisted the dumbwaiter up to its destination. Every whim, whether salmon soufflé or a bed of unblemished banana peels could be summoned with a snap of the fingers, eaten (or ignored) at leisure, and left on the table for someone else to clean up.

And you could hire someone like Ma to give their life over to you, while their own family got left with the scraps.

It went along like this, a month of carrot cubes and crusty pots and tea trays, until one Friday evening in October when Alphonse, the footman, wandered in. And spoke.

"Your mama," he murmured quietly, "she need you upstairs."

Alphonse was somewhere in his twenties, tall, clean-shaven, and just handsome enough to be pleasant to look at but unthreatening to the master of the house. He sported neat fingernails, a perfectly pressed uniform, and an elegant, vaguely French accent—at least, I thought he did, because he said as little as possible. In short, he dressed immaculately, spoke rarely, heard nothing, and glided through the house unnoticed. He was the ideal servant.

I shut off the water sloshing in the sink and wiped my sweaty forehead on the top of my sleeve.

"What, now?"

Alphonse just raised his eyebrows slightly.

I dropped the copper pan I'd been working on, the last one of the night, back into the sink and wiped my hands on my grease-spotted apron.

Alphonse looked pointedly at the apron. "But she say clean up," which was easier said than done. "It's time to meet your maker."

I froze. What shortcut or misstep of mine had been discovered? "She said," I squeaked, "it's time to meet my maker?"

Alphonse shook off the phrase with a quick toss of his head. "I'm sorry, my English. That is to say— your master. It is time to meet your master. You go to meet Mr. Sewell."

Mr. Sewell's office was as big as a ballroom (or so I thought, until I saw the ballroom), overlooking Central Park and anchored by an enormous carved desk and a Persian rug I expected could fly you to Arabia. I later learned that this had once been the library, which explained the floor to ceiling shelves lined with books in fancy leather bindings.

Mr. Sewell's desk was covered not with the classics,

but all the latest editions of the city's newspapers. It figured, as he owned one of the biggest newspapers in New York, the *Daily Standard*. We weren't much for newspapers in our house, though I loved to glance at the headlines on the *New York Graphic* or *New York Yodel*, which kept us up-to-date on what socialite had poisoned her lover or which politician was spotted in what speakeasy.

Ma had told me all about Mr. Sewell—how he lunched with the mayor, how he flew with Lindbergh, how the outlawing of alcohol in this country had him to thank—but what she hadn't told me, as he came around his desk to inspect me, was that he was an absolute dish. He was tall and broad-shouldered and with a face that I suspected Ma's romance magazines would call "chiseled." And when he looked at you, it was with these swimming pool blue eyes that made you wonder if he might not be a little bit in love with you, if you were someone else entirely.

So to think that my ma not only knew but was whispering with this titan of New York society—well, it was enough to set my knees to rattling.

After a few quiet words to Ma, Mr. Sewell strode over and shook my already-shaking hand.

"So, Martha, is it?" He towered over me, unwavering as a flagpole. "Welcome to the team. I call it a team because we're all in this together, making this a happy and efficient home. Aren't we, Mrs. O'Doyle?"

"Indeed we are, Mr. Sewell." My mother beamed.

"And this team needs strong players who are willing to pitch in and do their share, never looking for glory for themselves—only for the team. Am I right, Mrs. O'Doyle?"

My ma gave a little nodding bow. "Correct as usual, Mr. Sewell."

"Let me ask you a question, Martha," and here he settled himself on the edge of his desk. "Do you read the paper?"

"Oh, yes, every day, Mr. Sewell," I lied, and Ma frowned.

"So who do you like in this election—Hoover, or your countryman there, Mr. Al Smith?"

Everyone in our neighborhood loved Al Smith, New York's former mayor, a mick like us who, as a "wet" called for the end of Prohibition—for alcohol to be made legal again. You couldn't walk the street without hearing his campaign song, an old saloon favorite, "The Sidewalks of New York." But I looked at Ma before answering and saw that she shook her head, ever so slightly.

"I couldn't exactly say, Mr. Sewell."

Here he laughed and looked at Ma. "Here's the

problem with you ladies: you get the vote, but you don't necessarily get the brains."

I could only think of what wrath Ma would rain down on some poor neighborhood chump who said this. But here, in Mr. Sewell's office, she just nodded.

He turned back to me. "Hoover's who you want. He's got the vision our team needs. He's not going to turn this country back into a two-bit saloon."

Here Ma broke out into spontaneous applause. Ma may have marched for the vote once, but she'd marched for the Eighteenth Amendment to outlaw alcohol, too, and the fact that oceans of booze still washed over the country did nothing to dampen her ardor.

"Your mother understands, see? She understands what America needs to stay on the path to success. And what would that be?"

I was thinking of Daddo who used to say, "The parents of Success are a Little Bit of Luck and Not a Little Bit of Money," when Mr. Sewell jumped in again. "Vision! Why, look at my example. I started with nothing but a small newspaper, an inconsequential outfit in Poughkeepsie, bought by my father on a lark. But I had one single-minded vision. And now, that small outfit is the most important paper in the greatest city in the world!"

I guessed that if his father published newspapers "on a lark," then Mr. Sewell probably started out with a bit more in his pocket than vision. But I just nodded and said, "Yes, sir!" like a rescued urchin in a dime novel.

The master began to pace the room, his legs striding over the rug's bold motifs, like a giant overtaking continents. "And just by working here, you will have an advantage I didn't. You will do your job surrounded by success." He beckoned me to the window, where all of Central Park was laid out. "There's New York's jewel, available for your viewing any time of day. Do you know what the apartment block going up on Seventy-Sixth Street is charging for that view?"

I didn't, and anyway, I wasn't viewing anything from the bowels of the kitchen. But I just whistled under my breath. "That's really something, Mr. Sewell."

He put his hands on my shoulders. "Well, Martha, now you have your vision, don't you? 'The nearer we live to the source of wealth, the more wealth we shall receive.' Do you know what book that's from?"

"The Bible?" I ventured, figuring when someone asks you a question about a book, you should always guess the Bible.

He chuckled. "Not exactly. Why, take a look at all

these books," and he gestured dismissively to the volumes that surrounded him. "Thousands of dollars spent by my wife and her father, touring Europe, shipping back books and paintings and gewgaws like this." He plinked a bronze statue of a Greek god on his desk with his fingernail. "And yet there are only two books in the world any man—or girl—needs. You've guessed one: the Bible." Mr. Sewell sent an approving look at my mother. "And the other, from which my quote was drawn?"

"Erm, *The Lives of the Saints*?" That's what Sister Ignatius would expect to hear.

Here he grimaced. "No. It's *The Science of Getting Rich*. Science!"

"Yes, sir."

"*The Science of Getting Rich*—that book will tell you everything you need to know. Plenty of advice for good living in the Bible, too. Did you know Jesus was the world's greatest businessman? That's from *The Man Nobody Knows*, and you should read that, too."

"Oh, yes, sir, *The Man Nobody Knows*."

"Yes, sir, is right. 'Pluck, not luck' is what I always say. Let me hear it."

"Pluck, not luck," I repeated.

"Louder!" he rumbled from his gut.

"Pluck, not luck!" I piped up.

"LOUDER!" and this time, his roar filled the library, and I was afraid those hundreds of useless books would be rattled off their shelves.

I summoned up a roar to match. "PLUCK, NOT LUCK!"

Mr. Sewell burst into a laugh and turned to Ma, pumping her hand up and down.

"A fine girl, Mrs. Sewell, and we'll turn her into a fine American yet. Martha, I'm going to start you off with a leg up. What do you say to a raise?"

I looked excitedly at Ma, who had already promised I could keep thirty cents a week toward the bicycle I wanted.

"Oh, Mr. Sewell," Ma blushed, "sure, you're too generous. Just to take on Martha at all has been—"

He silenced her with a wave of his hand and dug into a pocket on his waistcoat. Into my hand he dropped two pennies, which clinked dully together, as if even they were embarrassed.

"Fourteen cents more a week, Mrs. O'Doyle; two cents a day for the *Daily Standard* each morning. See to it. Your daughter will have the vote soon enough, and she'll need the vision of my paper to keep her—and this country—on the right path."

"Oh, thank you, Mr. Sewell," I mustered, closing the two dull coins in my fist.

"Just remember, you may have gotten this job thanks to your mother, but you'll only keep it thanks to your own hard work. We reward dedication and commitment here, and shirkers will be shown the door, no matter who their parents."

As I backed out the door, as if leaving the presence of a king, I spotted yesterday's *Daily Standard* in a wastebasket. I snagged it and tucked the pennies into my shoe.

Pluck (not luck) was all well and good, but it did nothing to vanquish those carrot cubes and greasy pots and tea trays. The basement tedium dragged on without interruption for a week or two—until one night, with the last copper pan polished and shining and hung over the stove, my mother reported that Mr. Sewell would be dining at home that night. Late. With a guest.

Well, that's when the pots really started flying.

"Just some sandwiches," Mr. Sewell had said, but Chef started in on some kind of puff pastry and insisted I hack the bones out of a chicken. Then Ma started squawking about the dinner tray, which I guess I'd forgotten to send up.

A pile of unpeeled potatoes still loomed at my elbow, where hot oil drippings landed from Chef's scalding spoon.

"Why can't she eat whatever Chef's creation there is?" I whined. "Or we could give her some of the vegetable slop he made for lunch," I said, ignoring Chef's glare. "There's plenty of that left over."

"Shirkers will not be tolerated. That's what Mr. Sewell said, and he meant it. And so do I."

Ma was called off to supervise the table, and I managed to get Mrs. Sewell's dinner tray into the dumbwaiter and out of sight, freeing me to finish Chef's multicourse banquet for two, snatching bites of potato soufflé and rose-shaped slices of ham when he wasn't looking.

By the time dinner was handed off to Alphonse for serving and the pots had been washed, it was well past ten o'clock and I was dead on my feet. I felt like I was climbing Everest instead of the back stairs behind Ma, and as we left, I almost didn't notice the shadowy figure loitering just outside the servants' entrance. Instead of removing his hat as he entered, he pulled it further over his eyes and snub nose and pushed past us.

"Press for Mr. Sewell, ma'am," he muttered, and flashed something in his wallet at her. She nodded and let him proceed.

"Who was that?"

"One of Mr. Sewell's contacts," she said, shutting

the door firmly behind us, "and dinner guest, I presume. Many of the leads and stories he depends on take place behind closed doors." She looked up and down the street before stepping out on the sidewalk. "Discretion, my dear. That's the true secret to success in this job."

I fell asleep on Ma's shoulder before the train even left the Fifty-Ninth Street station. But around Thirty-Fourth Street, my eyes snapped open. In the distraction of the dinner rush, I'd sent up a nice, hot bowl of porridge to Mrs. Sewell, but I'd forgotten the fixings: no raisins, no cinnamon, not to mention any fancy sugar. I was about to tell Ma, who was nodding off herself, but then I thought of what Daddo would say: Don't tell the Devil good day till you meet him. So I let the swaying of the train rock me back to sleep.

Early the next morning, as I slumped waiting for the train and the day's drudgery, I dutifully peeked at the *Daily Standard*'s headlines:

HOOVER SHOWS VISION AT MILWAUKEE RALLY

'SOFT' DRINKS SALES SURE TO RISE

MIRACLE DRUG BUILDING INTEREST. . . .

But it was a headline on the *Yodel* that seized my
attention:

WILD ROSE'S WILD NIGHT

——

*New York's Most Eccentric Recluse Steps
Out—in a Dumbwaiter!*

——

*Nearly Burns Mansion to the Ground—
Accident or Arson?*

——

Chapter 4

I was relieved to find the Sewell mansion standing when we arrived.

Some smudges alongside the stove and a thick haze of smoke over the kitchen were the only evidence of Rose's wild night. Whatever had happened, nothing had burned to the ground, besides Chef's scrap bucket where a blazing rag seemed to have fallen.

Chef banged around the kitchen, furious to find his sanctum breached, ready to fend off any suggestion that it was *he* who left an olive oil–soaked rag too near a pilot light.

Upstairs was a symphony of slamming doors, books flung against walls, Ma's running feet, and above it all, Mr. Sewell roared out his ire in the form of un-questions.

"I want answers, do you hear me!" he roared. "Does no one here know one damn thing about what's going on in this house! Who is going to explain how this happened!"

I turned up the water in the scrub sink, but still scraps bounced down the servants' stairs—"outrageous," "disloyal," "leak," "like a sieve"—and I wasn't sure what angered him most: that his crazy wife had tried to burn the house down on her way to a midnight stroll . . . or that the *Yodel* had scooped it?

And how had they found out? I wondered as I washed the dishes from Mr. Sewell's supper. Once the food was on the table, the servants were expected to leave, to protect the master's privacy. Only Alphonse, who served at the table, would have stayed to the end. . . .

A ringing of the front bell brought a temporary stay to the storm upstairs. And a few minutes later, Alphonse entered the kitchen. Chef looked up, hoping for a luncheon guest. *"Non,"* Alphonse shook his head, and Chef flung a handful of *mirepoix* vengefully across the room.

"Who's here?" I asked Alphonse, grabbing a broom and dustpan to capture the tiny celery cubes.

"The doctor," responded Alphonse. "The *meesus* is foul again."

I wrinkled my nose. "Foul?"

"How you say—not foul, sick? The doctor wants some tea for the *meesus*. You make it."

"*Please*," I added in my head, as if correcting the twins. I put on the kettle and started a tea tray. "So what happened? You were here, right? Did the missus really ride in the dumbwaiter? Was she the one who set the fire?" I lowered my voice. "On purpose?"

Alphonse looked uncomfortable, but his eyes involuntarily flicked to the smoke-damaged range.

Did Alphonse discover the whole brouhaha while clearing plates to the kitchen? "Did you see the whole thing? Get over!" I punched him on the arm, which he frowned about and rubbed gingerly. "What did she look like? Was she nutty as a fruitcake? Was she foaming at the mouth?" A new thought occurred to me. "Was she trying to make something to eat? I'll bet she was, after all that mush day in, day out." Especially the plain porridge I'd accidentally served up.

I saw Alphonse recoil from my questions, as if he regretted the glance at the stove that had escaped him, maybe even regretted saying hello. He feigned either ignorance or indifference with a shrug and turned his back to me, retrieving a small book from his vest pocket to read while the water boiled.

Steam rose in me as it built in the kettle. To know what happened—to have been an eyewitness to the whole crazy scene—and to keep it to yourself! What was the point of knowing something if no one knew what you knew?

The silence expanded. Chef banged pans. I tried to catch Alphonse's attention again, clinking china and clearing my throat. Alphonse leaned back against the workstation, but said nothing. A hint of steam appeared. Alphonse flipped a page. When I peeked at the book, he shifted so his back was more squarely to me. I flung a pot into the scrub sink and smiled when he reached for a handkerchief to dab the dirty water off his uniform.

Finally the watched pot had boiled and the tea was made, a gingersnap added as a kind of apology, too little too late. I thrust the tray at Alphonse, who barely looked up from his book.

"No, it's for you. They ask you to bring it."

"Me? Why? When?"

"Be quick, they say. As for why——" He shrugged again slowly, but shot a look at the tea tray.

There is a step that a maid perfects in time, a step that is swift in speed, yet seems unhurried. It's a dance between you and marble staircases and un-secured rugs where you glide effortlessly, your tray virtually hovering.

But I had not perfected this and had to stop outside Mrs. Sewell's rooms to wipe off the saucer with my apron. It was only when I looked up that I noticed something strange on the landing: a cot, a washstand, a small table with a deck of cards in mid-solitaire.

The door opened up, and a wide, ruddy face popped out, like a tough working the door of a speakeasy. "What, girl?"

"They told me to come up!" I protested guiltily, but for what I didn't know.

"Agh, the tea. Well, bring it in then. Don't stand outside ogling."

The man flung the door open and stood aside.

My breath caught in my throat.

What lay before me was no lady's room. It was nothing short of a museum—or what I imagined a museum would look like. In just a small suite of rooms were crammed dozens of paintings, stacked three or four deep, leaning against walls or tables or wardrobes. Others were hung haphazardly, some big, some small, some dangling so they half jutted across a window, as if they were in a constant state of rotation, changed daily, hourly even, with every shifting mood.

No wonder she was nuts, I thought. The walls pulsated with life—no, with something larger than life. Gods and goddesses fought and frolicked. Dukes and duchesses followed me with their eyes. Winds swept through landscapes, and bowls of glistening fruit dangled out of reach. And in some pictures, lines shot this way and that, meeting nothing but squiggles and blocks of color. They added to the sense of madness, to the sense that every form of life had been sucked out of the house and stuffed somewhere incapable of containing its grandness. Like Mrs. Riordan's son, George, who wanders Willoughby Street claiming to be King Tut, Queen Victoria, or Heavyweight Champion boxer Jack Dempsey, depending on the day.

"Martha!" My mother's sharp call summoned me back to Mrs. Sewell's bedroom where a small crowd surrounded a canopied and curtained bed. I set the tea down on a marble-topped table, and when my mother gestured to stay, tried to will myself into the wallpaper.

"The dumbwaiter will have to be seen to," came Mr. Sewell's voice; he then raised it for another listener, as if speaking to a child. "You may always exit via the door, darling. You know we're longing for you to join us downstairs. But this dumbwaiter business, it's not safe."

"What has she been reading?" The scolding voice came from a distinguished older man standing at the head of the bed, one hand through the curtains and the other holding a pocket watch. A stethoscope dangled from his neck.

"The paper, mostly," my mother offered. "Mr. Sewell's, of course. It's good, sound thinking, and I believe it makes her feel—well, part of Mr. Sewell's world."

"Is that so?" responded the doctor. "It's good of you"—he raised his voice in that fatherly way, as Mr. Sewell had done—"to take an interest in your husband's affairs. But you should focus on your health at the moment. And what's this?" He put away his watch and picked up a leather volume from the bedside table. "Ovid? Classical literature for an invalid, for heaven's sake. And what's this—Dante's *Inferno*?" The doctor shook his head. "*Inferno*? And you wonder why she starts fires at the first opportunity?"

My mother cleared her throat. "She sometimes requests books from the library downstairs."

"From my office, you mean?" Mr. Sewell huffed and shook his head. "I should have sold off that library. I knew it the minute I laid eyes on it." I wondered if Mr. Sewell was mad that his wife wasn't reading *The Science of Getting Rich*. Then again, she was already rich, so maybe she figured she didn't need to.

"You can't!" hissed a voice from inside the curtains. "They're mine!" I saw a curtain billow out suddenly as if it had been kicked. The circle surrounding the bed widened for a moment, as everyone took a step back: Mr. Sewell, my mother, that flat-faced man who opened the door and now stood with his arms folded and feet apart, like a soldier at ease. I saw now that he wore some kind of all white uniform, almost like pajamas.

"No, no, this won't do." The doctor turned his back to the bed and addressed the others in the room. "Mrs. Sewell needs calming influences, not provocative material. Now," he rubbed his hands together, "what about yesterday? Any changes in routine? Is she still on the diet I prescribed?"

"Toast and tea, some broth at midday. And porridge at night, to make her sleepy, just as you prescribed." My mother waved me forward out of the shadows. "My daughter, Martha, made the porridge herself."

"It's too salty!" came the strained voice behind the curtains again. Which was just silly, if you asked me, considering the heaps of fancy sugar I poured into it.

But not last night, I remembered.

47

I stepped forward a bit to a spot at the foot of the bed where the curtains parted; a bedside lamp softly illuminated the inmate, the crisp sheets pulled all the way to her shoulders, as if straining to pin her down. Her thin, pointed face was framed by a halo of patchy hair like straw, clumped over the pillows that were piled behind her. Her eyes narrowed when she saw me, sizing me up, and when I met her gaze, a hand appeared from under the covers to scratch wildly at her cheek, which I saw was red and inflamed with a fiery rash. But as if fatigued by the effort it took to hold my gaze, her eyes fell to the silk coverlet.

"It's too salty," she insisted wretchedly.

I turned and gave a small shake of my head to the doctor, to show him that this couldn't be true. "It's just plain porridge, sir." When Ma looked at me strangely, I continued. "With raisins and cream and sugar, of course."

"Interesting. Another symptom." He stroked his beard, then took out a small notebook and jotted something down. Then he proposed lots of syllables, explaining that this was when the brain confuses two flavors or smells. "Could be a sign of seizures. Or a sensory hallucination, most associated with *dementia praecox*—schizophrenia, as it's also known." This last term I recognized as the one Mrs. Riordan used about George. "We may be drawing closer to a diagnosis," the doctor opined, raising one finger, "but we will never clarify what is the illness and what the disruption until we can provide an entirely calming environment for our patient."

"Doctor," interrupted Mr. Sewell, "there are days she doesn't even recognize me." He ran his fingers through his hair, and he looked less like a titan of industry than a lovesick schoolboy. "I wonder, are we doing all we can? Is this the right environment for her? I just wonder about the influence of these paintings."

"Yes, I agree. They're too stimulating, many of them." Here I caught the doctor eyeing a canvas where a half man, half goat pursued a particularly nimble and naked forest nymph. "Better that they be removed."

And here is where, as one would say, all hell broke loose.

Mrs. Sewell rose up on her bed like a demon, tearing down the curtains around her and attacking the doctor, her husband, even my mother, as one and all scrambled to simultaneously contain her and protect themselves from her claws.

The doctor produced a shot from his bag and,

with the help of the man in white, whose ham-hock arms were able to absorb her fury, injected Mrs. Sewell with something that transformed her from she-devil to blubbering mess.

"I had hoped we wouldn't have to do this again, Rose." The doctor shook his head.

My mother took the weeping Mrs. Sewell in her arms like a child, murmuring and smoothing her hair—like my brothers when they fell, I thought, and me too once—while the doctor gestured for the men to join him in the next room. I stayed frozen where I'd retreated near the door, just beyond their circle.

"Do you see her in there, crying like a baby, holding on to that maid like her own mother? Entirely necessary," the doctor opined. "Here we have a woman entirely alienated from her own femininity. I see it every day in my practice. Women given the vote, but not the judgment to exercise it. Women given an ounce of freedom, which they use to smoke and drink, to dance on tables! Do you see?"

"Quite so," interjected Mr. Sewell. "Why, I've always said—"

"When women think they're equals to men,"—I was impressed to see that the doctor's self-importance did not shy even for my employer's—"like men, they will gravitate to what is attractive and easy, and society will lose its moral center." With a deep sigh, the doctor produced and popped in a peppermint, like an orator after a great speech. He turned finally to Mr. Sewell. "Now, Archer, I know that you are anxious to speed your wife's path to recovery. And yes, while there are many excellent facilities—why, we Americans are at the forefront of modern psychiatry! The forefront, I say!—Mrs. Sewell's best chance at recovery lies at home. For it is here that we must help her reconnect with her femininity. Her mother died when she was young, yes? So let her be mothered again"—my own mother stepped into the circle at just this moment—"here in her childhood room, and she will mature into a true woman again."

"Yes, but what about these paintings?" interrupted Mr. Sewell. "They're making her crazy."

My mother broke in with urgency. "I've promised her they won't be moved. They may not provide the calming environment we hope for, but the prospect of their absence is far more disturbing to her than their presence." She seemed to only realize her boldness, as she ducked her head, casting her eyes down, away from her employer. "I'm sorry, Mr. Sewell, it's just I'm sure it's the right thing for her."

"She has a point, Archer," the doctor murmured from the notes he'd started scribbling.

Mr. Sewell's face froze for a moment, the dam of his composed face holding back his irritation at being disputed. After a pause, he bowed lightly. "You're right as always, Mrs. O'Doyle. As Dr. Westbrook says, the important thing is to keep Rose calm. And happy. There's no rush—that is to say, we mustn't rush the process."

"Well." The doctor tucked his notebook in his pocket and then patted my mother on the arm. "You are a good role model for her now. By withdrawing from the world"—Dr. Westbrook had begun packing as if onstage in front of his audience, and I shifted to relieve my weary lower back—"she has retreated back to her infancy, returning to seed, as it were. Let us nurture her; let us give her the peace she needs to sleep through this winter of the soul. When she is ready, she will reemerge and blossom in her full womanhood."

Ma nodded, and finding me in the corner, indicated I should follow her out. We descended silently, step by step, back to the servants' quarters, and when we reached Ma's office, really the former housekeeper's sitting room, Ma closed the door behind us and sank into a chair.

"Gee, is she always so——"

My mother just held up a hand to stop me. "What did you do?"

"I didn't do anything. Probably what happened was—"

"Please, no lies this time. What did you do?"

I looked down at my hands, which twisted my apron into knots. "I forgot the sugar," I mumbled.

And with this, my mother dropped her head into her hands. I noticed for the first time traces of gray shot through her hair.

"I'm sorry, Ma! It won't happen again! I'll make sure . . ."

When she looked up again, her eyes were red. "She's a shadow of the girl I first knew. Once she was resilient, unstoppable, a force of nature, that's what she was! And now the least change in routine sends her into a tizzy. All the strength and life drained out of her, or worse, distorted in these bizarre outbursts! And whatever we do—the sleep therapy, the restraints, the baths—she just fades more and more into the shadows." She wiped roughly at her eyes with her handkerchief. "Mr. Sewell says we should stay the course, listen to the doctor, but I'm starting to believe we won't ever get her back."

Ma indulged her sorrow a few moments more,

then blew her nose and tucked her handkerchief away. As she rose to splash her face with water from the washbasin, she said, "Go home, just go home. Tomorrow you'll work upstairs, as a parlor maid. I can't chance any more changes to Miss Rose's diet or routine."

I ascended out of the basement to a glorious autumn day in New York, the sun shining and a free day ahead of me.

So why did I still feel such subterranean misery?

Because my carelessness had gotten me in trouble—again.

Because I'd caused Ma such grief—again.

And that grief wasn't even for me.

Chapter 5

Despite my free pass to play hooky, something more attractive beckoned me: sleep. It had been weeks of up at dawn, an hour on the train, on my feet for ten, sometimes twelve hours, followed by another hour on the train, and practically collapsing on our house's stoop. I understood now Ma's "weekly holidays," her two hours every Sunday afternoon, napping and reading in bed while I kept the twins out of her hair.

I dozed the whole train ride home, dreaming of a proper kip on the sofa and an after-school runaround with the twins. But the door was open and lights on when I got home. Which meant no afternoon nap. It meant something much better.

Daddo was home.

Daddo was what everyone in the neighborhood called him, short for Daddy O'Doyle, from when I was a wee thing and he'd show me off at the saloon. When Ma thought he was perambulating me around the park, he'd roll me instead into Gallagher's place, sit me on the bar, and we'd do patty-cake and handy-dandy-sugar-candy. And everyone would roar with approval and stand him a pint and tell him we should go on the road together, Daddy O'Doyle and his Delightful Daughter.

His back was to me in the kitchen, and as I threw my arms around him, I felt through his coat how thin he'd gotten on the road. The scent of his hair tonic wound its way into my nose. Still Brilliantine.

He spun around and snatched me up, getting crumbs in my hair from the soda bread he was eating. "Marty, my pearl!"

This was in the days when a Brooklyn pearl sounded like poyle and boil like burl.

"You're supposed to be, that is, I thought you were at school. Could it be you're playing hooky, you scamp?"

I pushed him into a chair at the kitchen table. "Don't eat standing up; you're getting crumbs everywhere, and you know what Ma will say. Let me fix you something. When d'you get back? How long are you staying? You know I'm a kitchen girl now? Well, I was. I can make you some eggs, some potatoes. I can run out and get some sausages." I pulled the empty Ovaltine jar where we kept grocery money off the shelf and started to dig around the bills.

He popped up again and went to the icebox, where he took a swig straight from the milk bottle. "No, no, don't go to any trouble, pet. I'm due back on the four o'clock train to Syracuse."

I sagged against the kitchen counter. "Four o'clock? You won't even see the boys."

"How are the rascals?"

"The same. I think, the same. I mostly see them when they're asleep, now that I'm working." I sighed. "They're such angels asleep."

"Ah, so not the same at all." He winked.

I laughed. "No, I suppose not. How are Creak and Eek?"

"The talk of Wisconsin!" Daddo did a little soft shoe on the linoleum, two imaginary skeletons on his side. A few years ago he beat a guy at cards who was an orderly at a teaching hospital. He couldn't pay out, so he stole a male and a female skeleton for my father instead, whom Daddo christened Creak and Eek. He designed this kind of marionette-ventriloquist frame that made it look like they were dancing and talking alongside him. "O'Doyle and His O-mazing Spook Show" was born.

"We sold out our Lake Superior tour, and now the Lake Ontario crowd got wind, so we're heading up-state on the silo circuit. Halloween time's always big for the skeletons." Daddo wrapped the rest of the soda bread in a napkin. "Mind if I take this for the train?"

I took the napkin from him and laid the bread flat on the counter again, slicing three more pieces which I spread thickly with butter and mustard and laid on with ham. Then I wrapped the whole thing back up in the napkin with an apple and a couple of Italian cookies Mrs. Annunziata brought back from her niece's wedding and put it back in his hands.

"So you'll be back after Halloween?"

"That depends on the box office, don't it? The more the folks want Creak and Eek, the less you see your dear old Daddo." He tucked the dinner bundle into his suitcase, sprawled open on the kitchen table, then started to buckle the straps. "Trust me, it's good that I'm gone so much. Means more money in the till."

I leaned back against the kitchen counter. "So stay a few more hours. When the boys get home from school, we can take them for an egg cream. Or stay till evening, and when Ma gets home we can go to the pictures. You can take a Pullman sleeper car upstate and sleep on the train."

The well-traveled suitcase swung from my dad's hand, his limbs already in motion. "Can't do it, dearie. I've got to swing by my agent's on West Twenty-Eighth before my train. Harry Beecham owes me for the last two tours, and I'm not taking no for an answer this time." He snaked an arm around my waist and pulled me in for a kiss on the head, then produced the Ovaltine jar from behind my back. "Tell your ma I'm taking a few shekels to tide me over," he said as he dug in. "Harry'll have a check here by the end of the week. Next week, tops."

"I'll tell her, but you know she'll be sore."

"Ain't she always?" He winked again. "You know what the Presbyterians say: You're damned if you do and damned if you don't."

"Yeah, well, we ain't Presbyterians."

"Then you should know, a good Catholic always asks forgiveness, just never permission." And with one more wink, he was gone.

I didn't bother telling the twins that Daddo had "come and gone," as they'd say. I gave Mrs. Annunziata the day off and treated them to egg creams myself, then let them play at the park all afternoon, while I dozed on a park bench. On the way home, I bought them gingersnaps for dinner.

"Ma used to get these for us," said Timmy, spraying cookie crumbs all over his school uniform.

"Yeah, but I like Mrs. Annunziata's cookies better," answered Willy. "She makes them herself. Why'd you have to pick us up?"

"Gee, thanks, pal. I thought you missed your big sis, or does Mrs. A. give you noogie kisses, too?" I planted a kiss and drove my nose into the top of his head at the same time. The boys loved-hated it.

Willy squirmed away, but smiled. "Nah, it's good to have you around, I guess. But why couldn't Ma come home, too?"

"She's busy."

"She's always busy," observed Timmy.

"Or tired," added Willy.

"Or crabby," said Timmy.

"Always crabby," nodded Willy.

Before, I would have joined in: Yah, Ma's worn down to the bone. Ma's dead on her feet. Ma's on the warpath.

But now that I felt busy, tired, and crabby, too, it didn't feel right to slag off Ma for the same. So I summoned my last bit of energy instead. "If it's yer ma ye be wanting, it's yer ma ye'll get," I bellowed in a grand exaggeration of my ma's brogue, "but sure, I'll be beatin' the divil out o' ye two with this here wooden spoon," and I brandished a stick I found on the ground. The boys screamed with delight and bolted for the corner.

The boys easily outran their tired old sis, and by the time they reached our front door, I was a half a block behind. Assured they'd gone inside already, I stopped to catch my breath at the corner, in front of the newsstand, where Mr. Conescu was packing up the morning papers.

The *Daily Standard* was still out, and I picked up a copy to read, as Mr. Sewell had instructed. "You got two cents for that?" Mr. Conescu asked. "It's still Saturday, on my watch." I put it back and just browsed the headlines:

COPS BEAT BOOTLEGGERS BACK

SMOKELESS CIGARETTES? SIR WALTER TOBACCO SAYS YES

AL SMITH "WET" BEHIND THE EARS . . .

But my attention soon turned to the *Yodel*'s front page, still with its Wild Rose headline, and while Mr.

Conescu's back was turned, I flicked the front page over to the story inside.

With all of the city's pleasures just outside her door, what drew Wild Rose to the kitchen last night? Midnight snack, joyride, or something more sinister? Our sources inside that secretive citadel tell us—

"Hey!" shouted Mr. Conescu. "What'd I say?"

I dropped the paper and trotted off before Conescu could squeeze me for my hard-earned pennies. But the article had confirmed what I suspected. "Our sources." So Mr. Sewell was right; there was a leak inside the house. And with only one servant present at the time of the escape, there was only one reasonable suspect: one tight-lipped footman, who may not speak much to me, but sure didn't mind squawking to the *Yodel*.

Chapter 6

Ireported to my first day on the job as a parlor-maid with a brand-new apron and a new sense of optimism. For whatever there was to do upstairs, it couldn't be harder than kitchen work, and at least I could catch a stray sunbeam falling in through the windows.

That was before I knew how busy Ma intended to keep me. I think she figured it was the only way to keep me out of trouble.

You couldn't blame her for trying.

My responsibility was the whole of the downstairs and halfway up the grand marble staircase. Magdalena, the other chambermaid, started at the landing and continued on up to the second floor. I did my best to be friendly when I ran into her at that midway point, with a "Hiya" and a "Some day, hey?" But she never moved her eyes off the rag before her. Ma claimed Magda, a recent immigrant from Poland, understood well enough to decode "dust this" or "sweep that," but I was starting to think she spoke no English at all. Or that maybe she pretended not to, saving her from any questions (or answers) about that strange household.

The third floor, happily, was mostly closed off, and the top floor was just Mrs. Sewell and that burly nurse-babysitter, Mr. McCagg, on the landing. My mother alone took responsibility for that floor.

One floor for one hearty girl might sound reasonable, but mind you, this one floor included an imposing entry hall, a reception room, a music room, a dining room, a ballroom, an art gallery. All of which was stuffed with carved furniture and expensive baubles from the Pritchards' many trips to Europe, where Rose's father tried to import class and stature by the boatload. Now all those items just drew dust like flies to a dung heap.

Bridie was the first-floor chambermaid sent downstairs to take my spot in the kitchen. I could only imagine the kitchen would be the better for it, as Bridie told me she "loved a good challenge" and scoffed when I showed her the soap pads. "With copper pots, you've got to use lemon wedges dipped in salt. And my secret ingredient: elbow grease!" She laughed like this was a joke out of the funny pages. "You'll see. You've never seen a pot sparkle till it's met my magic fingers!" Chef nodded admiringly and set aside three petit fours for her. I left them both to all the fun they could find at the bottom of the slop sink.

Why I was cleaning at all was a mystery; none of the rooms ever seemed used. Besides his furtive, late-night dinners, Mr. Sewell didn't care to entertain in the fashion of the society set. "He's a businessman; he's too busy for all that," said Ma, adding that he often said he'd prefer a penthouse in one of those new luxury apartment buildings going up on Fifth Avenue, with "none of this frippery to look after."

I worked my way slowly through the rooms in Ma's prescribed rotation—the front parlor on Mondays, the dining room on Tuesdays, and so on—when Ma discovered a spilled drink in the art gallery. It must have been left over from Mr. Sewell's supper with his reporter two nights before, the night of Mrs. Sewell's dumbwaiter incident. In all the excitement, it had gone unnoticed, and now the parquet floor underneath it was likely warped and discolored. While Ma went to telephone a woodworker, I hauled a mop and bucket in.

The gallery led from a reception room to the ballroom, a long, wide promenade, with tall ceilings and a barreled roof. It was designed, it seemed, for partygoers to take in the impressive collection of artworks as they moved from cocktails to supper, and the room was dotted here and there with sofas and lounges, so that guests might relax to better enjoy.

What exactly? Like the rest of the house, the walls were empty. Well, nearly empty—at one point there must have been dozens, maybe even a hundred paintings crammed along those walls—the ones, I realized, that now populated Mrs. Sewell's rooms upstairs.

Today there were just four. They were hung along one side, neatly in a row, as if someone had begun planning an exhibition and then lost interest. Each was draped with a sheet, protected from my unworthy eyes.

The spilled drink in question was located halfway between these sole survivors. The drape to one painting had been pulled aside, dragging halfway on the ground. I felt a shiver, as if witnessing the scene of a crime. I could picture Mr. Sewell strolling here with his dinner guest, stopping to show off the artwork purchased by his once charmingly cultured wife, then dropping a drink (of club soda, no doubt) in surprise as smoke and a bloodcurdling scream emanated from downstairs, from the kitchen, from the . . . dumbwaiter?

Shards of broken crystal littered the floor like a land mine, a warped circle outlining where the melting ice and liquid had seeped into the inlaid wood. A few flying shards had landed as far as the half-pulled drape, where the sheet pooled on the floor. I'd have to shake it out—without pulling down the painting behind it.

I stood back to assess the job. The painting was tall, high, much taller than me, and the sheet clung to its top right corner.

And behind the sheet, beckoned two hands. Delicate and white, with long tapered fingers, one circling the wrist of the other, which clutched—what exactly?

With my thumb and forefinger, I pulled back the sheet a bit more, revealing an apple, held possessively, close to the chest.

Now I gave the sheet a billowing yank and found myself face-to-face with the most beautiful woman I'd ever seen.

Eve. The apple said it all.

Poor Eve, I thought. In every stained-glass window and Bible picture, she was always cold and naked, a fig leaf stuck to her nethers, shoving an apple into Adam's mouth. Or she's only slightly more covered in animal skins, as God banishes her from the garden, following Adam with the requisite weeping and gnashing of teeth.

Also, she always has a belly button, which just makes no sense at all, if you think about it.

But this painter—an Italian guy, ROSSETTI, the little brass label read—lavished his Eve with a rich peacock green fabric that spilled around her like a waterfall. He'd chosen the color to match her intensely serious blue-green eyes, and against it the apple seemed frankly dull in comparison. It was some kind of apple I'd never seen before, which made sense because everyone knows the best grocers are always Italian.

Another thing I liked about this Eve is that Adam was nowhere to be found. I'd never seen a painting of just Eve alone before. Come to think of it, she usually appeared with the subtlety of a moving picture actress, batting her eyelashes at Adam or wailing behind him or letting herself be sweet-talked by the villain-snake. But here she was lost in her own thoughts, looking so fixedly at something beyond me. And instead of foisting the apple on Adam, she held on to it, like it was hers and hers alone.

Maybe if she'd kept all that knowledge to herself, I thought, there wouldn't have been a Fall. After all, it was Adam who spilled the beans to God.

"What are you doing in here?"

I whirled around. Alphonse's head was peeking through the double doors.

"Ma sent me in." I rattled the glass shards in my dustpan. "To clean up a spill."

"Ah." The head disappeared back into the hall, then reappeared followed by the rest of Alphonse's body. His long legs had him standing by me in an instant. "You look at the paintings." He said it as an accusation rather than an observation.

"The sheet fell off," I lied automatically.

But he wasn't listening. He was looking, too.

"It's Eve," I broke the silence. "See the apple?"

He laughed loudly. "That one is not Eve."

"It is so," I retorted. "And I should know, after eight years of Catholic school."

A sound escaped the side of his mouth like a deflating tire. "You think you are the only Catholic? Where I come from, it is not just school. We are fermented in it, like wine."

"Where's that exactly?"

He ignored me. "That is no apple. And that is no Eve."

"Not an apple!" I guffawed. "What is it then, I'd like to know?"

"Americans." He shook his head. "You know nothing but catsup and Cracker Jacks."

"That's rich!" I shot back. "When the French eat snails! And frogs!"

"The legs of the frogs," he retorted coolly, as if this explained it all. "And as for the lady in the painting," he continued before I could get another word in, "you do not have to wonder. Her name is right at the top of the painting."

He was right. At the very top, several lines of verse appeared as if written on an old-fashioned scroll. I tiptoed up to see, but it did me no good.

"It's in some other language."

"True," he shrugged. "Not so difficult if you read Italian."

"And you do, I suppose."

He shrugged again. "But you do not even need language to unlock this painting. All you need to know is in the picture itself."

Before I could ask him what he meant, a click of the door admitted Ma and her businesslike step. "Aren't you done yet? Why is that drape off? Alphonse, what business do you have here?"

Alphonse immediately took up the drape and, after shaking out the glass gingerly in the direction of my dustpan, tossed it back over the painting. I in turn scrupulously swept up the chards.

"The young lady could not reach the top. I was helping."

Ma looked at us suspiciously. "Well, now you've helped enough. There's no one on the door, and Mr. Sewell wouldn't like it, especially with all the trouble we've had."

Once the doors were closed behind Alphonse, Ma turned back to me. "I don't like you speaking with him."

"Don't worry, Ma." I kneeled down to sweep the last of the glass. "He barely talks anyway."

"Still. I am quite serious on this. There's to be no fraternization on my staff."

"I've got no idea what that means, so I can't imagine I'll be doing it."

"Enough of your sass. It means chatting up the fellas, and it's a one-way ticket out the door with no reference letter."

I nodded, although I knew this was an empty threat, as Ma was the one who'd be writing my reference.

"And don't go touching the paintings." The drape had slipped again, and Ma reached out to fix it, then stopped and pulled it back just as I had. "These are Miss Rose's pride and joy," she murmured, gazing at the beautiful lady, "and her ticket in."

"Ticket to what?"

"To New York society. When Mr. Pritchard and Miss Rose moved from West Virginia to New York, no one would give them the time of day, no matter how much money they had. So Mr. Pritchard took Rose to Europe, 'to get cultured' he said. Came back with all this art, all the books in the library, even designed this house to accommodate the haul and the folks he hoped to attract—the gallery, the ballroom. Used his railroad connections to get a private railway platform in the basement, to lure society types direct from their country houses upstate."

"Did they come?"

"Oh, land, yes! Half the social register turned up for the teas and dinners and dances, eager to see the fancies. And it worked. Between her father's money and my dress skill, all the most eligible society bachelors came 'round to court her," Ma said with certain pride.

"Including Mr. Sewell?"

"Well, yes," she said shortly. "Of course."

I looked around the room, with its empty walls and draped sofas. "So? Where is everyone? All these society types?"

She cleared her throat. "Miss Rose's father died shortly after her marriage. Miss Rose hoped to step in and take over her father's affairs, but that was absurd for obvious reasons."

I nodded as if I understood what those obviously absurd reasons were.

"Some nephew took control of his company instead and managed to bankrupt it in short order. After that . . ." Ma paused. "Well, Miss Rose had always been . . . saucy, but after that, her behavior grew increasingly strange. She insisted on bringing all the art up to her rooms, refused to come out. All those newfound friends stayed away—not such friends after all, I suppose. And now, this"—Ma tossed the drape back over the lady in blue, turning her into a ghost again—"is all that's left."

"Still!" she turned back to me with a pasted-on smile. "As they say, there's no friend like a faithful servant."

"But you said she took all the paintings upstairs," I said while sucking the finger I'd nicked on Mr. Sewell's crystal. "So, what about these?" The four frames huddled together, abandoned, on the gallery wall.

"Occasionally," Ma sighed, "Miss Rose gets it in her head that certain paintings need to be downstairs. For Mr. Sewell's visitors. So she'll direct me to bring this one or that one down." She peeked under the drape again. "Come to think of it, it's been donkey's years since she had me switch them out. Maybe she's finally grown tired of the whole exercise." Ma slid the sole of her shoe around the floor until she found a stray shard. "You'll need to sweep this whole area again. We can't have visitors slicing their slippers on glass."

I slid my foot, too, mimicking with the toe of my boot. "Wouldn't a bit of linseed oil treat this spot? At least, as a measure until the woodworker arrives?"

Ma thought for a moment. "Yes, I believe it would. Good thinking, Martha. There's some in the supply cupboard." She checked her watch. "I have to run to meet with the grocer. When I return, I want the spot treated and the room vacated. Understood?"

I nodded and watched until the door closed behind her with a shudder of glass.

The linseed oil was instantly forgotten as drapes were whisked away from each of the cloaked paintings, sheets piled on the floor.

It was an odd collection of paintings, there was no

denying it: some larger than life, some small enough to tuck under your arm and walk out the door.

I also saw that, for a woman who ate only broth and mush, Mrs. Sewell seemed quite obsessed with fruit.

The painting next to Eve—or whoever she was—dulled in comparison, a ho-hum looking bowl of fruit, dusty, patchy apples in a pile, and here again was that strange-looking apple I'd seen in the lady's milky-white hands. *Nature morte*, a title on the frame read; the name on the frame was Courbet, and then the words: *in vinculis faciebat*.

The painting next to it was quite pleasing. *Still even,* the plaque said, by Willem Kalf. Large, imposing, and undeniably rich, it made me think of the dishes that came down after Mr. Sewell's more indulgent dinners: half-finished crystal glasses of wine, a mussed tablecloth, crumbs on the table and silver decanters overturned. But something about the way this one was painted made the whole scene seem delectable rather than messy. The silver glinted, the fruit shone, the linen tablecloth beckoned, and I impulsively reached out for it, feeling silly when I discovered it cold and flat against my finger.

The showpiece against all the finery was that fruit again, and now I had to admit Alphonse was right—

this was no apple. The fruit had split open as if exposing its guts, an explosion of glossy red. Against the soft white linen tablecloth, a single scarlet, glowing seed had fallen, and the maid in me wanted to sweep it into my dustpan.

The whole display felt obscene somehow, though I couldn't for the life of me figure out why. It was like it was something impossibly rich and lush, and yet at the same time . . . too much. Just looking at it gave me something of a stomachache.

And what was "still even" about it? I had no idea.

The final painting also baffled me.

Unlike the previous picture, there was nothing rich or delicious or enticing here. Instead the small canvas—I could pick it up easily, if I'd wanted to—mashed up a confusing maze of shapes and lines and smudges of brown, gray, and orange, like a subway train at rush hour. Black seedlike dots speckled the scene here and there. Above the action hovered the hazy words *cafe 3*, like a shop window shining through the fog.

Was this malarkey supposed to be a painting of a café? I looked closer.

But the title, next to the painter's name on the frame (Pablo Picasso), explained nothing: *The Pomegranate.*

Chapter 7

That night I dreamed of the beautiful lady.

I hadn't dreamed at all since I started working at the house—too tired, probably, falling into what Ma would call "the sleep of the dead."

But that night I dreamed.

I was in the house's lavish courtyard—it seemed I couldn't even escape the house in my sleep—where all the trees and shrubs had been draped in white sheets. From beneath one, two milky-white hands appeared. They held that strange fruit, and when I reached out for it, placed it safely in my own chapped hands. But as I raised the fruit to take a bite as I would an apple, it burst open, spewing the seeds, the juice staining my apron, dripping between my fingers like blood.

When I woke up, I swore I could taste that juice—both tart and sweet—on my tongue.

"Do you really speak French?"

I was supposed to be beating rugs behind the house that day, but it was raining, a steady November rain that drowned the autumn leaves, so I'd been given permission to dust the front parlors instead. I spent an hour on the front reception room alone, waiting to catch Alphonse at his station in the neighboring foyer. But Alphonse had been sent on some errand, and just when I thought I might dust the end tables down to wooden nubs, he returned to his post.

My question must have startled him, because he froze, his face drained of color.

I stepped out from the shadows and held up my dust rag, as if showing I wasn't armed.

He finally cleared his throat and answered, "Of course."

"Courbet"—I pronounced it Cor-bett—"it's a French name, right?"

Alphonse's shoulders dropped and he let out a breath. "Ah, so you were looking at the paintings?"

"'Course. So is it French?"

"Yes. Yes, he was a French painter." Alphonse seemed

to warm to his subject. "They call him a 'Realist.' He wanted to paint what truly was, not what the people want to see."

"So," I fished in the pocket of my apron for the note I'd scribbled after closing up the gallery, " *'nature morte'*—what does that mean?"

Alphonse looked down the hall, back toward the servant stairs. "I do not think your mother wants me talking to you."

"Don't worry," I said, settling myself in a chair easily worth more than our house on Willoughby Street. "Ma's doing the inventory with Chef downstairs. They'll be ages."

Besides, I'd tried asking Ma about pomegranates and *nature morte*, but she'd just looked at me strangely and asked if I'd finished sweeping out the fireplaces.

Alphonse looked unconvinced, but after a moment he plucked up the rag I'd left on the table and made himself look busy by polishing some candlesticks. "*Nature morte.*" He said it with more flourish than me. "To translate, dead nature."

I thought back to the painting with this title—just a bowl of fruit. Dusty maybe, but edible, I thought. "That doesn't make any sense. Everything in the picture was alive. Well, at least, it wasn't dead."

"It is just the French way of saying what you call in English," he paused with his rag, searching for the words, " 'stop life'—a painting of objects. No people, no animals. Nothing moving. All still."

"Oh."

"Still!" He smiled broadly, as if he had solved a nagging problem. " 'Still life.' That is the name. Not stop. 'Still.' "

Alphonse shot another look over his shoulder. Hearing no footsteps approaching, he continued his lecture, all the while staying with his busy work, moving beyond the candlesticks to the table. "Yes, because in Dutch, it is *still even*. Did you see the Dutch? These were the masters of the still life."

" 'Still even.' " I remembered those words on the opulent table scene. "Does that mean dead nature, too?"

"It means 'still the same.' Always the same. Frozen, maybe one might say. The Dutch had this belief of death and life together. Did you not see spots on the fruit, the beginning of . . . how do you say, rotten? Of mold? You will always see these things. It means that . . . ," the rag paused on the table as he stared in the distance, putting together some idea in his brain. "It means that something is beautiful from a distance, but once you go close you will see the flaws." He began polishing again. "And that nothing, even the most beautiful, lasts forever."

I hadn't noticed rot or mold or flaws. But those bloody red seeds returned to my mind, and I shivered.

"So that is what they mean by these paintings." Alphonse stood up, now looking at me with curiosity. "And the Picasso, what did you think?"

I shrugged. "A bunch of nothing and a name that doesn't mean anything."

"If it was truly a 'bunch of nothing,' it *would* be nothing—a blank canvas. No, Señor Picasso chooses the colors, the shapes for a reason." He stopped, something on the leg of the table catching his eye. He spat on the rag and knelt down to set to buffing it out. "Nothing on that wall is an accident."

"You mean, on the painting?"

"I mean on the wall. And *The Pomegranate* is indeed a name that means something, especially on that wall."

Alphonse's rag kept moving, so I kept talking.

"So what is a pomegranate anyway? And, oh!" I consulted the paper scrap again. "*In vinculis faciebat.* What's that?"

"It is Latin. It means 'made in prison.' And as for

what is a pomegranate," he spat on the rag again, then shook his head forlornly. "Pomegranate—a fruit. But a very," he searched again for the word, "specific fruit. Specific for a reason. Not that you Americans—"

"I know, Cracker Jacks and catsup. Y'know, this is all awful fancy talk for a footman. French, Italian, Latin. How many languages do you speak anyway? And how'd you learn so much about pictures? Were you a priest or something in the Old Country? Because for someone so highfalutin', you'd think you'd have a job that didn't bring you so low."

Alphonse stopped rubbing. He slowly stood up and tossed the rag, spit and all, on the table, then walked out of the room.

As usual, I'd pushed too far, driving away not only the serving staff's resident language expert but one heck of a parlormaid.

But just as I was reaching reluctantly for the spittled rag, he returned, his usually placid jaw clenched.

"There is not a thing that I know that I did not learn from a book," he launched in. "Maybe you do not know what this is. They are this big, white things in the middle—"

"I know what a book is."

"Do you? Perhaps they have forgotten what you

look like. There is an excellent library full of these books, just over there." He indicated the direction of Mr. Sewell's office. "Homer, Herodotus, Virgil, Ovid." He paused, then repeated. "Ovid. Words written many thousands of years ago, but they are still available to anyone—a millionaire, a lady, a footman, even a maid."

I didn't recognize half the words in his little speech, but I did recognize a dare when thrown in my face. And that name—Ovid—sounded familiar, but I wasn't sure why.

I faked a guffaw. "Available to everyone? Really? Not when that library is in Mr. Sewell's office. Which is always kept locked, I believe?"

Alphonse stuffed his hands in his pockets and rocked back and forth in the doorway. "There is one person in this house who stands guard at the door. One who meets the postman every day, takes the post, and places it on Mr. Sewell's desk. For this job, he is trusted with a key. And this person, he is very worthy of this trust, but sometimes, maybe he does not always remember to lock the door behind him."

As he turned on his heel, I heard a jingling of keys from somewhere in his pocket. And then, farther down the hallway, the unmistakeable *click* of a lock turning.

Ma and Chef were still doing the inventory. Mr. Sewell was at the newspaper offices, and Magdalena was silently working her way through the second floor. Alphonse was now nowhere to be seen.

In other words, there was no reason—outside of it being absolutely, entirely, and indubitably forbidden— not to go in the library.

I tiptoed over to the doors. The knob turned with an easy *click*, and without even a look over my shoulder, I slipped in.

No longer filled with Mr. Sewell's outsized presence, the room felt cavernous.

Bookshelves covered three of the four walls, shadowed as the storm flung leaves and twigs in staccato against the park-facing windows. The wall switch flipped with a sharp *click* that made me jump, and the electric lights overhead shone a garish spotlight on the walls of rich leatherbound volumes—brown, red, green, like the wet leaves stuck to the windows.

While handsome, those neat rows of satiny spines made finding a particular book near impossible. There were no titles imprinted, no authors listed, no labels on the shelves indicating History or Philosophy or Greek Mythology, and on closer inspection, there were many gaps and breaks in the shelves' soldier-like order.

A large ledger lay open on a stand in one corner which seemed to hold the key to the mysterious collection. It looked like each book had been added to the catalog as it was purchased. The catalog showed the bulk of books dropped in one go at the beginning and the rest added chronologically. But each was then shelved according to a numerical system with unhelpful tells like 876.544F.

This system meant that there was no alphabetical order to guide me to Ovid, whoever or whatever that was. It required going through the ledger, page by page, starting from the beginning.

Luckily I found several books identified as Ovid early on, part of that first haul from Mr. Pritchard's European travels of 1910 (so the ledger said).

But to the right of most entries, I saw my mother's long, looped handwriting: "Removed by Mrs. O'Doyle, for Mrs. Sewell." March 3, 1927. April 4, 1926. October 2, 1925. The dates were scattered like seeds across a span of the last few years.

And then I remembered where I'd heard that name, Ovid, before Alphonse. It was the book the doctor noted on Rose's bedside. The book, he suggested, was too provocative, too stimulating for such a fragile woman. Maybe any woman.

Was the doctor right? Was this Ovid helping to drive Mrs. Sewell crazy?

Maybe the words in these books were some kind of ancient spell, I mused as I hunted for the number (873.01), where the Ovids were meant to be found. Maybe they were designed, when read, to scramble your mind or spark an insane frenzy,

True to the register, in a section with a small brass plaque labeled 870-880, half the shelf was empty. I eyed the ransacked shelf with suspicion. Maybe an ancient spell wasn't entirely believable. But then what could be so dangerous here? And what was the subject that held Rose's fascination? Art? Botany? Fruit?

I warily plucked up one of the leftovers.

The soft, expensive leather gave nothing away, but after a few brittle pages Ovid's name was revealed, followed by *Fasti*, as if this explained anything. I flipped to the middle:

> ". . . When from her saffron cheeks Tithonus' spouse shall have begun to shed the dew at the time of the fifth morn, the

constellation, whether it be the Bear-ward or the sluggard Bootes, will have sunk and will escape thy sight. But not so will the Grape-gatherer escape thee . . ."

The doctor might be right about the books. Writing like that would drive anyone crazy.

I tossed the volume back on the shelf and grabbed another: *A Commentarie and Arguement, Most Humbly Submitted, on a Translation of the Most Noble Verses, Metamorphoses* . . . The title dribbled over at least a page and maybe into two. This book at least contained pictures, although not even in color: just black-and-white block prints.

As I flipped the book open, it fell to the center plate.

Here I saw a girl clinging in terror to a rock, shinking away as a scaled creature rose out of the waves that crashed at her feet, his talons threatening to rip open her flesh.

On closer inspection, I saw that she was actually chained to that rock, with no chance of escape.

I quickly turned the page.

The next illustration was no better. Here a creature hulked over a waif of a girl, cornered in the dead end of an elaborate maze. Some kind of half-

and-half monstrosity, with the body of a strong and strapping man, but the head and feet of a snarling bull: it was labeled *The Minotaur*. Teeth bared, horns glinting, he drew upon the quivering maiden.

But I never found out what happened next because with the sound of the library door swinging open, the book dropped from my hands.

"What!"

Just that one word, in Ma's mouth, said everything.

(This is the problem with books. When they're bad, they drive you away with their forthwiths and thithers, and you'll never finish them, no matter how much your teacher harangues you. But when they're good, they lure you in and won't let you go, and that can get you into just as much trouble.)

I snatched up the Ovid and shoved it back on the shelf, whether in the 100s or 900s, I didn't know or care. From my apron pocket I produced that spitty rag and began frantically polishing the books with Alphonse's saliva.

"I was just walking by, and the door was open, and I was going to close it, but the books looked so dusty. I mean, look at that dust . . ." I coughed, I thought, convincingly. "And we're all a team here, aren't we, so I just thought I'd pitch in."

"That's rubbish. This room is *never* left unlocked. Unless . . ."

Her eyes narrowed a bit, and I did feel bad that Alphonse was going to take the blame.

"Locked or no," she continued slowly, "you should never enter this room without permission. There's not just the matter of Mr. Sewell's private papers. Each one of these books is worth a month's wages, some more. If you so much as ripped a page . . ." Ma left the thought unfinished, a ripped page an unspeakable offense.

I took a step back from the bookshelves, now afraid of even accidental contact. "No wonder Mr. Sewell wants to sell them." I whistled under my breath. "Not that he needs the money, of course."

"Mr. Sewell's financial decisions are no concern of yours," Ma snapped, but then paused. "But it's like Mr. Sewell said, I suppose: living near the source of wealth—well, we could all learn from his vision."

Ma crossed over and withdrew my hastily shelved book.

"I'll have you know it's not that Mr. Sewell doesn't care for the books. Heavens, no! One of the most cultured, most learned men in New York, Mr. Sewell is! It's that, as he says, these books could be working for him, instead of him for them. If he sold them, he says, he could put the money in the stock market and double it overnight! With all the information that flows into the paper, Mr. Sewell is always the first to hear of any stock tip." Ma nestled the book back into its proper place in the 800s. "I've been thinking of putting a bit of money in the market myself. With Mr. Sewell's guidance, of course," she murmured to herself.

I stood back and looked at the sea of books. Each one worth at least forty dollars, times what? A thousand, and then that doubled in the market . . . "So why doesn't he sell them?"

Ma stood back, glancing over the stacks to make sure all was in order.

"They're not his to sell; they belong to Miss Rose. The books, the paintings, the house. They were all left to Miss Rose by her father. So as long as she chooses to keep them, Mr. Sewell is their keeper and protector." Her eyes passed from one end of the bookshelves to the door. "And hers," she murmured.

She put her hand on my shoulder—a familiar grip the twins and I called "The Claw"—and began to steer me back toward the door. "And as his deputy, it's up to me to see that all is maintained in the same condition in which it arrived in this house. Which means"—here she pushed me out into the hallway

and stepped out behind me, blocking the door—
"no unauthorized visitors. And that includes you."

She turned back, and with her own jangling ring
of keys, which dwarfed Alphonse's, she turned the
lock with a definitive click.

And that was the end of Mr. Sewell's library,
for me.

Chapter 8

That night on the subway home, I scanned the car for *Daily Standard* headlines while mentally depositing two pennies in my own Ovaltine jar.

There wasn't much to hold my interest (**"TROY MOTOR COMPANY STOCK CLIMBS" "INTEREST RATES RUMORED TO DIP"**), so I leaned back to read the *Yodel* over the shoulder of the engrossed office girl to my right. Today's top story was a corker: A chorus girl from the Follies had been caught in Montreal with a congressman, pretending to be his wife. The real wife reportedly got wind and took off the next day for Reno for a quickie divorce, with a Portuguese waiter in tow. And now the chorus girl's mother was suing the congressman for kidnapping. A delicious, scandalous mess, the whole thing.

By the time I got home, I couldn't remember what was so interesting about pomegranates and Ovid anyway.

And Mrs. Sewell, if I thought about it.

Did anyone care what made Georgie Riordan think he was King Tut? No, they just tipped their hats to him on Flatbush Avenue and told his ma "no charge, ma'am" when she came into their store. What made me think it was any stranger for a rich person to go loopy than some joe from the neighborhood? If anything, in that house filled with books of monsters and paintings of squiggles, it made *more* sense.

So let the lady of the house lie in bed, eat porridge, read about half men–half goats, and stare at pictures of watermelons and alligator pears. Whatever the source of Mrs. Sewell's troubles, I wouldn't discover it in all the myths of Ancient Greece and Rome combined.

At least, I was pretty sure.

"Land, the racket, Martha!" Ma flew into the Sewell music salon, where I was cleaning the piano's keys, approximating Gershwin (I thought) in the process. "Though at least the noise led me straight to you. I need you to run an errand."

I had my apron off before Ma could even give

me a destination. After a week of rain, the light glimmered and danced outside, and it was exactly the kind of day I would have faked a stomachache at school and headed to the park or the beach or simply anywhere.

"I see the schemes in your eyes, young lady, and you'll be wise to check them right there before they meet up with your brain." Ma took the apron and looped it back over my neck, spinning me around and tying the strings together with a yank. "You'll be in an official capacity, a representative of the Sewell household, and I expect you to comport yourself accordingly."

I loosened and retied the strings around what Daddo called my jelly belly. "All right, all right. Where to?"

"Mr. Sewell needs this note hand delivered to the Dukes. It's got to get there right away, before Mr. Duke leaves for their golf game. Mr. Sewell can't make it, you see. It's just a bit farther up Fifth Avenue, across from the museum." She stared in my eyes. "Shouldn't take you more than fifteen minutes. I'd go myself, but I must go downtown and give the grocer a what's what. And Alphonse . . ."

"Ma, I've got it!" I snatched the letter out of her hand. "Across from the museum, easy."

Ma took a deep breath, looking like she'd already regretted the decision. "Can I trust you on this, Martha?" She looked over her shoulder, and I knew she was wondering if the silent-but-compliant Magdalena was within shouting distance.

"Of course!" I jumped in her line of sight, to block any further thoughts of Magdalena. "Just a trot up Fifth Avenue and back. What could be easier?"

To my credit, I skipped straightaway to the Duke place, strangely pleased to find their fairy-tale mansion slightly smaller than the Sewells'. But any haloed grandeur I felt was in my own mind alone, because the footman refused to even open the front door to my maid's uniform. He met me instead at the servants' entrance, where he took the letter between two fingers and coldly closed the door in my face.

But even that couldn't get me down. It was one of those delicious fall days in the grand finale of the season: sun beaming through the branches, just a few golden leaves left clinging, its red and orange sisters already carpeting the ground. I inhaled deeply, drawing in the toasted scent of sunbaked leaves, the smoke of fireplaces coming back to life. The clean, cold bite of winter was waiting in the wings.

Across the street from the Dukes' was Central

Park, where I could take the long way home through the tree-lined paths and promenades. Hop through a game of jump rope. Maybe get a last Italian ice before the pushcart vendors closed up for the season. With Ma oblivious downtown, there was no rush.

There was only one thing standing between me and the park: The Metropolitan Museum of Art.

The museum, an imposing matron of a building, took up nearly two blocks along the other side of Fifth Avenue, guarding any view of the park. As I strategized which side to go around, it felt as if it were daring me to pass, like a playground bully exacting a toll of milk money.

I deliberated at the foot of its grand stone steps, waves of well-dressed art lovers streaming up and down past me: the kind of folks, I thought, who had nowhere to be on a Wednesday but in front of a painting. People who probably looked at paintings every day of their lives—and not just four, once, for a few minutes before the drapes were pulled over them.

People, maybe, who knew about pomegranates and Ovids.

A gaggle of girls, dressed in starched and pressed school uniforms, jostled me as they swept up the steps. One gave me a look of annoyance—most likely the same look she gave her own maid, her own Katie or Mary or Bridget at home. Before she asked them to go dust her own paintings—but not look at them.

I stuck my tongue out at the girl's back as I mounted the steps behind the class trip. I'll just take a quick peek, I told myself. It won't take but a minute.

The inside of the building was bigger than even St. Patrick's Cathedral, where I'd stop in occasionally with Daddo to light a candle for a new gig. Maybe this is what the swells worship, I thought, as my eyes traveled from the enormous sprays of flowers to the soaring roof: beauty. And old things. And the money to buy both.

And yet, its grandeur felt strangely familiar. No more or less opulent than the Sewell mansion, the museum was merely bigger and more crowded. No wonder all the rich folk looked so comfortable here: It reminded them of home.

But my familiarity ended there in the center hall, as I watched couples, class trips, and retired millionaires wander in all different directions. Which way to the paintings, I wondered? And what did it cost to see them?

"You look lost, dear."

A voice came from what I saw now was a desk in the middle of the hall—INFORMATION, a sign read.

"I'm not lost," I shot back at the disembodied voice. "I have a right to be here." But even as the brash words left my mouth, I wasn't so sure I did. So far in this place I'd seen socialites and school groups, but no other unaccompanied maids off the job.

"You don't need to snap," came the gravelly voice again, and as I looked more closely, I saw a pompadour of gray hair hovering behind one of those giant floral arrangements. "I never said you didn't. The Metropolitan Museum is open to all, no matter one's station."

I peered now over the desk and saw a little old lady perched on a stool, her hands on a cane. She dressed like pictures I'd seen of Queen Victoria, all puffy sleeves and lace and high collars. "I only meant"—and as she resettled her hands, I saw that her gold cane topper was as big as a doorknob—"that you look as if you don't know where to begin."

"Do you work here?" I asked, realizing how silly the question was as soon as I asked. Ladies this old and rich didn't work.

She guffawed, too, at the very idea. "I am a docent." In my silence, she continued, "I guide patrons to the works they seek." And as I continued to look blankly, she kept going. "I help people who come into the museum. Now, what are you looking for, dear?" Her lined face was haughty but kind, like a queen distributing Christmas baskets to peasants.

What was I looking for? Even here and now, I wasn't sure. A knowledge of art, so that I wouldn't have to keep asking Alphonse and feeling stupid? I probably couldn't cover that in a quick fifteen-minute trip. An understanding of what it was about the pictures that made Mrs. Sewell so crazy?

I needed something I could see quickly. Something that would shed light on one tiny sliver of this strange story I'd found myself in.

"I'd like to see the pomegranates, please," I said loudly, as if it were the most natural thing in the world. A couple standing next to me, consulting with another docent about "naturalism" (which was a thing to see, apparently), turned to stare.

The old lady blinked. Paused. "Pomegranates," she repeated finally.

"Ye-ess," I faltered a bit. "Just . . . whatever pomegranates you have around."

She blinked again. Then she shifted her weight slowly forward, reaching some shelf below and producing a map that revealed the museum to be a labyrinth of interconnecting rooms. She also produced a fountain pen, which hovered in the air over the map. Then, before she could circle whichever room held the fruit pictures, she set the pen down and pushed herself up to her feet.

"Follow me, dear," she commanded, slowly lumbering her way toward a side hall. A guard stood at attention, but with the faintest wave of her wrinkled hand, he stepped aside.

My feet slowed. Gallery after gallery telescoped behind the guard, and I knew the wise thing would be to say a polite "Thank you anyway," and hustle my way back down Fifth Avenue.

Sensing my hesitation, the old lady paused and shot back over her shoulder, "I said, follow me."

So I did.

It was a good idea, at least in theory.

I thought, maybe if I saw all the art with pomegranates, I would detect some kind of meaning that tied them all together. That would explain what about them fascinated Mrs. Sewell.

Also, how many paintings of pomegranates could there be in this place?

As it turned out, a lot.

Not just paintings, but sculptures, jewelry, pages

from books, furniture, even hieroglyphics from the tombs they were excavating in Egypt that very moment, shipping back crates of slabs with carvings like the funnies—many of which included pomegranates.

And here's the thing: Every one was in a different room. Or hall. Or wing. Each of which required a walk between them. A walk that became a journey behind the old lady's unhurried hobble. The sound of her brass-tipped cane striking the marble floor echoed throughout the galleries, but she didn't seem to mind. In fact, I'd say she took it as her birthright.

Along this expedition, the lady—"Mrs. Harry Ellsworth, née Edith Inness, how do you do"—filled the time with a slow but constant stream of opinions. Somehow I couldn't get a word in edgewise, as she condemned some industrialist's shockingly "paltry" donation to the museum, and compared some painter she thought was a "fraud" to another she found "sublime," and complained how her daughter was marrying "the wrong sort" of man. (Whoever he was, I guessed he would be considered very much the right sort in my neighborhood.) One thing was for sure: Mrs. Harry Ellsworth was not a woman to be interrupted.

So I listened and I followed at a glacial pace, shuffling my feet alongside hers. Each room came with a story, a whole oration of history and religion and wars and wardrobes, in which each pomegranate came delivered.

And every time the story around that little fruit changed, the meaning changed along with it.

So for the Egyptians, the pomegranate suggested success and prosperity. But for the Greeks it was the fruit of the dead.

In ancient China, they thought it brought lots of babies, while in India, it was a cure for diarrhea.

The ancient Hebrews used it to represent the fertility of the Promised Land. But they also suspected it was the forbidden fruit that got Adam and Eve kicked out of Eden.

Mrs. Ellsworth lingered on one painting—"Italian Renaissance, dear"—and nattered on about perspective and modeling. I just saw a naked baby Jesus, a halo tipped off the back of His head like a silver dinner plate, straining out of the Virgin Mary's arms. The object that drew His attention turned out to be a book (I guess reading at under a year was another of His miracles), which He studied with the same focus Daddo gave the day's racing form.

Just to the right of His chubby elbow was an open

pomegranate. "An emblem of the Church," explained the label next to the painting, "a symbol of both Christ's crucifixion and resurrection." Life and death, all mixed together. As I drew closer to inspect it, I saw that its seeds were scattered along the table. But unlike the dark glistening seeds of Mrs. Sewell's painting, these looked pale, somewhat dry, a listless pink.

The more I walked, and the more Mrs. Ellsworth talked, the less I understood about the pomegranates. Depending on where I looked, they were sometimes juicy, sometimes dusty. Sometimes the seeds looked like gems, sometimes like blood, sometimes like small insignificant pebbles. Sometimes they meant life, sometimes death, and everything in between.

It seemed that the pomegranate could really mean anything. Which meant it meant nothing.

We finally found ourselves back in the great entrance hall, where, without any paintings or sculptures to prompt a lecture, Mrs. Ellsworth finally stopped to place her full attention on me.

"So, dear," she said, settling back onto her stool behind the desk, "was that enough pomegranates for you, then? Did you find what you were looking for?" She studied my uniform with narrowed eyes. "Which household are you with, did you say?"

As part of New York's Fifth Avenue set, Mrs. Ellsworth surely knew the Sewells. Or knew of them, at least. And just as I was about to open my mouth, I remembered what Ma said: Discretion is the heart of a good servant.

Then again, would I be at the museum right now if I were a good servant?

Whatever my motivations, I had no trouble answering the question. "I work for the Duke house. Just across the street."

Here's something you may not know: There are no clocks in the Metropolitan Museum.

I realized this as I stepped back out onto those majestic steps and found the sun dancing along the treetops in the park. It must have been at least four o'clock, I realized in a panic, and no matter how long Ma's errand downtown would take, it would be over by now.

As my feet flew down Fifth Avenue, all the useless pomegranate-stained knowledge tumbled around my brain: life and death and seeds and orbs and babies and poo.

But what did it all mean to Mrs. Sewell? No matter how many pomegranates I saw or cultures I visited, none of it changed what it meant to one lady in her own strange reality.

I was flying past Seventy-Eighth Street when, out of the corner of my eye, something stopped me in my tracks: a fruit peddler across the avenue. He was packing up his cart with a forlorn look, his long beard not quite covering the soup stains on his waist-coat. Business was bad today, he shook his head, bad every day if he was honest. Maybe another corner, another neighborhood. I cut him off, and delight-edly he told me he had what I was looking for. Left over, he said, wrapping it in a brown paper bag, from some recent Jewish holiday. It felt a bit mushy in my hands, but it would do.

I was just going to open it, see the real appearance of the pomegranate's seeds for myself, place one on my tongue and . . . what? Bite down? Suck until it disappeared like a candy button? Would it be juicy? Hard? Tart? Sweet? I slipped quietly through the ser-vant's entrance and headed for the kitchen, passing Ma's hat and coat already hung on her usual hook. I cringed to think how long they'd been there.

"Martha O'Doyle!" Bridie tutted as I plucked up the sharp knife at her elbow. "Now where have you been? Your ma has been searching high and low all afternoon for you."

I stopped, the knife tip poised on the fruit's flesh.

"What do you mean? Wasn't she at the grocer all day?"

Bridie giggled. "No, silly, just until noon. She was called back; Mr. Sewell has a new guest tonight. I heard it might be Clara Bow!"

I groaned loudly enough to make Chef holler I'd make his soufflé fall. "You covered for me, right?"

"Why, no, I said I had no idea where you were!" She nudged me gently out of the way as she hoisted up Mrs. Sewell's supper tray—the sweetened tea, the sweetened porridge. "Really, I was so worried about you!"

I'd have to come up with a really good story this time. Maybe something about a subway track fire. Or a lost orphan. I hadn't used that one yet.

"Where were you anyway?" Bridie slid the tray into the dumbwaiter, then stopped, taking in my strange fruit. "Out shopping for produce? You know we order in all the marketing."

I looked at the pomegranate still held firm to the cutting board. Suddenly I had no interest in seeing its glistening, glimmering guts.

But then I had another idea.

"This," I shoved the pomegranate into Bridie's hands. "It's for supper. For Mrs. Sewell. Ma asked me to get it." Bridie blinked. "As a treat," I finished.

"Oh, well then, thank you! What an interesting addition. How do I prepare it then?" Bridie questioned cheerfully. "Shall I slice it for her, or perhaps I could—"

I grabbed it away, searching and finding a small, deep bowl, which would keep the pomegranate from rolling away. "Like this," I said, placing the bowl on the tray and closing up the dumbwaiter. "Just . . . just like this."

And before Bridie could ask any more questions, I pulled the cord, pulled and pulled and pulled it, sending the fruit to its destination in the sky.

What would that simple red globe mean to Mrs. Sewell? Heaven? Earth? Life? Death? Or simply a snack?

Would it be the very thing she'd been craving, hoping for, obsessing over? Would it cure her of her obsession, bringing her confusion to an end?

Or would it set off an episode that would make the Night of the Plain Porridge look like a tea party?

For the next hour, I alternated between being chased out of the kitchen by Chef, playing Cat and Mouse with Ma, and sneaking back down to the kitchen again. When I heard the squeak of the dumbwaiter descending past the first floor butler's pantry, I flew down the stairs again.

"Mrs. Sewell did *not* care for that fruit, I can tell you."

I pushed Bridie out of the way (in true Bridie fashion, she apologized to me: "Oh, so sorry, I'm so clumsy!") and snatched back the pomegranate.

Bridie was right. The fruit was still where I'd placed it on the tray, unopened, mushy and unappetizing.

But then I picked it up. And I saw that Mrs. Sewell had done the same.

And with small, shallow nicks—pressed in with a fingernail, it looked like—she had spelled out a single word:

HELP.

Chapter
9

Sunday, for me, was no day of rest.

When I was in school and it was just Ma who worked, Sundays started early. With Daddo always on the road, it was up to me to give Ma a break. I'd let her sleep in a bit and help get the boys ready for Mass, which meant twenty wriggling toes to stuff into four stiff shoes and one million hairs to plaster down, each one pointing a different direction. Then there was Mass itself which our Father Riordan seemed to want to wrap up as quickly as we did, but it still meant forty-five minutes of distracting the monkeys so Ma could listen to the homily.

Then we'd all pitch in—well, Ma and I would while the boys snuck away to play army men under the bed—on all the cleaning that'd gone undone all week. After that was Ma's "Sunday holiday." This was Ma's one and only luxury in life: an hour or two in bed, her corset discarded, a pot of tea and *Jane Eyre* near at hand.

I was charged with keeping the boys out, and when I was younger, chasing the boys through the rain or bracing myself for another snowball fight, I resented Ma's laze abouts. Now that I, too, had spent from Monday dawn to past-dusk Saturday on my feet, I should have demanded a holiday of my own.

But now a day running after the boys felt like a lark compared to a day up to the elbows in Murphy Oil Soap. I thought through our usual Sunday haunts: the stickball game on Willoughby Street, the empty lot where you could shoot bottles with Jimmy McGarry's BB gun, following the drunks as they left Donovan's speak, hoping for falling pennies.

But the fall weather had taken the weekend off, allowing winter to visit in its absence, and the gray skies and biting wind were conspiring to drive us inside.

"Aw, sis, this place is lousy. Whadda we s'pose to do here?" Timmy whined loudly.

Though I'd never entered its halls before, something about the library made me shush my brother with a rap on the head. It wasn't so much the quiet or the other patrons as the dark wood and hanging brass lamps put me in mind of being in church.

"Nah, Tee, you got it all wrong." Willy had already pulled a reference book off the shelf and was preparing to rip a page right down the middle. "Lookit all the paper airplanes we can make."

"C'mon, Dubs, that won't work. Put some spit on it!" Timmy jumped in when the page stayed fast.

"Hands up!" I broke in, and both boys reached for the sky, like cornered gangsters, knowing from Daddo that a dawdling response would mean a slap on the head. I swiftly cleared the table of all books, the one I'd gotten from the librarian safe under my arm. "You're in a library for pity's sake. Keep up the roughhousing, and you'll get raw chicken for dinner like the junkyard dogs you are."

"I wanted to go to the pictures!" Timmy huffed. He'd gotten the idea somewhere that my newfound wages were earmarked for his pleasure budget.

As usual, Willy joined in. "Me too!"

"Well," I settled myself in a chair at the table, "what I'm going to read you—"

A chorus of wails went up, with responsive shushing from the room's occupants.

"*Read you*," I repeated, "has more thrills and chills

than the latest Douglas Fairbanks picture!" Under my breath I muttered, "I hope."

So far, my forays into the Sewell library and the city's museum had yielded no keys or clues, just story after story, whose meanings shifted with the story-teller.

But there was only one storyteller whose story mattered. And so far, her only writing was a single word, pressed into produce with a fingernail.

HELP. The word followed me around the house over the next few days, tapping me on the shoulder as I cleaned from room to room. As I mopped the hallway outside the gallery, I felt those grand, expensive paintings held the secret to something. Something dark and threatening. And the pomegranate was at the center of it.

Of course, I couldn't dismiss the idea that maybe Mrs. Sewell was afraid of pomegranates full stop. She was crazy, after all. But if she were, I thought as I rubbed Brasso onto various shiny gewgaws, would she pick it up, write HELP on it? Why didn't she tantrum, throw it across the room, cower in a corner in fear? No, she picked it up thoughtfully, used it to write a message, not even knowing who was at the receiving end of it.

Whatever it was about pomegranates, they had to

stand for something specific—not to Egyptians, or Indians, or chubby baby Jesus, but something specific to Mrs. Sewell.

And I had nothing to go on but four paintings about pomegranates.

Well, almost nothing. There was one other thing: the book on her bedside table by someone named Ovid.

I needed to connect the dots somehow. I needed to go somewhere where I could find all the stories I needed without keys or admission fees or fear of Ma walking in.

The public library.

And thankfully, here a sweet young librarian, with only *pomegranate* and *Ovid* to go on, directed me to *one* story. In a book called *Metamorphoses*.

Apparently it detailed various Greek types and the ways they changed into other things. "Like a caterpillar," the pretty young librarian said searchingly as she put the book in my hands. "Metamorphosis, yes?"

The term sounded familiar, and I had a vague memory of copying it down from the blackboard in Sister Catherine's class that spring we hatched and released butterflies.

Looking at the book and all its big words made me feel I was in the presence of something—not holy exactly, although I had some urge to cross myself. So I settled the boys, made them sit up, wiped the mustard off their cheeks. And read:

> Not far from the walls of Enna, there is a deep pool. There, it is everlasting spring. While Proserpina was playing in this glade, and gathering violets or radiant lilies, Pluto, almost in a moment saw her, prized her, took her.

"See," I tapped the book, "kidnapping, boys!" Timmy lifted his head up from the table, where he had pretended to fall asleep. I continued:

> The frightened goddess cried out, and the flowers she had collected fell from her loosened tunic. The ravisher whipped up his chariot, and urged on the horses through deep pools and sulfurous reeking swamps.

"What's sulfurous?" broke in Willy.
"Smelly," I responded, "like a lavatory."
"Ewwwwww," Willy reacted with a disgusted smile.
"Waitaminute," broke in Timmy. "I saw this same

story last week at the picture show, but it was starring Mary Pickford, and they were in the Wild West."

> Meanwhile Proserpina's mother, fearing, searched in vain for the maid.

"Hey, she's a maid like you, sis!" snickered Willy. Then came a whole subplot about a nymph who turned into a pool of water, which lost the boys to a discussion about whether they'd ever seen a mermaid. I flipped ahead until I found the mother, named Ceres, again.

> In her anger, she dealt destruction on farmers and the cattles in their fields, and ordered the ever-faithful land to fail. The crops died as young shoots, destroyed by too much sun, and then by too much rain.
>
> Then the water goddess Arethusa lifted her head from her pool, saying "O great goddess of the crops, I saw your Proserpina. She was sad indeed, but she was nevertheless a queen, the greatest one among the world of shadows, the consort of the king of hell!"

"Marty said a bad word," Willy sang gleefully, craning his head around so that the entire reading room could share in their disapproval.

I plowed on.

> Ceres rose in her chariot to the realms of heaven. There, her whole face clouded with hate, she appeared before Jupiter.

"Who's Jupiter?" Willy again.

"The king god."

"God the King? Where's Jesus?"

"No, Jesus isn't in this one." I gritted my teeth. "Just listen."

> "Jupiter, the daughter I have searched for so long has been found. If only Pluto will return her!"
>
> And Jupiter replied, "Proserpina shall return to heaven, but on only one condition: that no food has touched her lips, since that is the law, decreed by the Fates."

"What kind of law is that—you can eat anything?" broke in Willy again.

"Same kind as we have now 'cept you can't

drink anything!" retorted Timmy. "In't that right, Marty?"

"It is, in a fashion. Now listen, this is the gist of it.

> Jupiter spoke, and Ceres felt sure of regaining her daughter. But the Fates would not allow it, for the girl had broken her fast, and had pulled down a reddish-purple pomegranate fruit from a tree, and taking six seeds from its yellow rind, squeezed them in her mouth.

Here it was. I sent Willy for the *P* encyclopedia.

> Now Jupiter divides the year equally. And the goddess, Proserpina, shared divinity of the two kingdoms, spends so many months with her mother, so many months with her husband.

I looked up from the book. Timmy's gaze jumped between me and its pages expectantly.

"And?"

"And," I closed the book slowly, "that's it. I guess."

"So she never escapes? She just has to stay down there in—"

117

"Hades," I finished as Willy arrived back from his encyclopedia errand, ears open to what he'd missed. "And the story says she gets to leave half the year."

That answer satisfied the boys, especially when they discovered that the following page included an engraving of Proserpina with a rather close-fitting tunic. Their attention was then entirely directed to finding illustrations of unclothed maidens, so I left them to the Ovid. That left me the *P* encyclopedia, and sure enough, Alphonse and the Metropolitan Museum were right: a pomegranate was no apple. The illustration showed the fruit split open, its seeds like teeth spilling out of a monster's mouth, calling to mind Mrs. Sewell's painting of that luxurious table, with the single seed threatening to stain the white tablecloth.

In Classical mythology, read the encyclopedia, *Persephone—also called Proserpina—is doomed to spend half the year in Hades after eating six pomegranate seeds, and it is this time that is said to account for the winter, or fallow, season.*

I sat back, and the boys pulled the volume out of my hands, giggling as they hunted for other words beginning with *P.* The feeble light from the high windows drew my eyes up, the only view the now-bare branches, blowing wildly and scratching at the glass.

Did Mrs. Sewell see herself as a real-life Proserpina? It made sense, in a way. Her early years sounded like a perpetual springtime of fun and capers. But now she seemed to be imprisoned in a winter of her own mind.

The question was: What had she done—what "pomegranate seeds" had she ingested—that doomed her to this life?

The boys wore me down with their crabbing, so I relented and took six bits out of my wages for the picture show.

We missed half of the live act, but it was just a couple of klutzy tap dancers who couldn't hold a candle to Daddo's Creak and Eek routine. Then there was an Oswald the Rabbit cartoon that already seemed obsolete; the papers said there'd be a talkie cartoon out next week called *Steamboat Willie*. Then there was a Three Stooges that had the boys laughing so hard they spat our their Goobers, which annoyed me plenty as that was their supper.

The newsreel kicked off with Tuesday's presidential election. The boys joined with most of the audience by hooting and booing and throwing popcorn at Herbert Hoover on the screen, and I didn't stop them. When Al Smith came on, we all joined in singing "The Sidewalks of New York," drowning out any predictions that Hoover would win by a landslide.

The feature, *The Racket*, was quite the caper, about a gangster pretending to be a model citizen; a cop, two newspaper guys, and a nightclub singer join forces to take him down.

The boys and I had quite the shoot-out on the way home, with Timmy and Willy expiring with great flair about a dozen times each. And after I tucked them in, first checking them all over for gunshot wounds with tickling fingers, I fell asleep with that picture show and that Greek myth all tumbled together in my mind, with bowls of fruit shot up by tommy guns, their sinister seeds spilling out on the sidewalks of New York.

Chapter
10

I wasn't the only one with gangsters on the brain that night.

The next morning Ma and I arrived to discover a scrum of reporters on the sidewalk—not in front of the Sewell house, but next door, in front of a swish apartment building that had recently gone up on the bones of a collapsed mansion. A handful of cops held the jostling mob at bay.

Ma went over for a quick word with a reporter, then made a beeline, tight-lipped, to the servants' entrance. Inside she set me to work on a catalog of chores before I could ask any questions. Whatever was going on outside had no effect on today's to-do list.

I was set to work straight off mopping that long marble hall that led from the front foyer all the way to the central courtyard. I started at the front door, hoping to find Alphonse at his station, where I could needle him for the full story that Ma refused to give me.

Unfortunately Alphonse was nowhere to be seen.

Although, I realized with a smile, that meant no one was manning the front door.

I laid my mop aside and seized the giant brass doorknob with two hands, hanging my weight on it to twist and swing the solid oak behemoth, then the wrought iron and glass outer door, on the hinges.

I was lucky that one of the cops from the building next door was going on break, crossing in front of the house at that moment.

"Pssst," I waved him over. "Officer! What's happening over there?"

"Haven't you heard?" His accent identified him as a fellow from our neighborhood back in Brooklyn. "Arnold Rothstein was shot last night."

"Who?"

"Doncha read the papers, kid?" Would everyone stop asking me that? "A gangster, one of the biggest. Bootlegging, racketeering, and, uh"—he blushed and tipped his hat to me—"other vices. The guy who fixed the World Series back in 1919! But you know what the Good Book says: You live by the sword, you die by the sword. Remember that, kid." He tipped his hat to me again and strolled on, in search of a cup of coffee, on the house.

I closed the doors, practically trembling with excitement, and made my way back to my mop. A real-live gangster, living right next door! Did Mr. Sewell know? Was gangland violence making its way to the Upper East Side? As I swabbed my way down the hall, my head swam with shoot-outs, tommy guns, getaway cars fleeing down Fifth Avenue, and mob molls on the stoop, chewing gum and cracking wise. Wait till I told the twins—they'd insist on joining me at work the next day, even if it meant picking up a mop themselves.

I was halfway down the hallway, just in front of Mr. Sewell's office, when I heard the explosion.

It wasn't much of a bomb, the cops said, only some cheap Chinatown gunpowder mixed with ingredients found in any closet of cleaning supplies—basically, an oversized firecracker. But it was strong enough to shatter the glass on the outer door. (The wrought iron was fine.)

From the scraps of brown paper and string, they said it was a package bomb—wrapped and disguised to look like an ordinary parcel. Nothing had been on the steps when I'd last peeked out; my blood ran cold to realize it must have been placed there mere minutes—even seconds—after I went inside.

I stood frozen and clutching my mop for safety, as the rest of the house came running past me: Ma, the other maids, Mr. McCagg from upstairs, even Mr. Sewell, who, as it turns out, had been working from his office at home.

In fact, Mr. Sewell ran directly out onto the steps before the smoke had even cleared, with no regard for his own safety. He brushed off the cops and stomped out the few smoldering embers scorching the marble steps with his fine wingtips, while his employees cowered just inside, in the foyer. I tiptoed up to join them, the fear of missing out greater than my fear of being blown to bits.

Mr. Sewell was holding up his hands to quiet the reporters around the steps, who, giddy with the promise of a terrific news day, had abandoned the Rothstein building and now pulsed around him, snapping photos and flinging questions.

"Mr. Sewell, do you have reason to believe the bomb was related to the Rothstein shooting?"

"Was the attack intended for you, sir?"

"Was it a revenge attack, sir? From Sacco and Vanzetti supporters?"

Sacco and Vanzetti? I looked to Ma for an explanation, but her stone face revealed nothing.

But even without reading the papers, I knew the names. Everyone did.

Sacco and Vanzetti were two Italian immigrants who tried to rob a factory in Boston and shot a couple of people in the process. A lot of people said they were innocent and the papers were prejudiced against them because they were Italian. Everyone was suspicious of Italians in those days—they were anarchists or terrorists or bombers, they said (although that hardly described Mrs. Annunziata to me). But innocent or guilty, last year they got the electric chair, so I guess it didn't matter what people thought. It was all over Mr. Conescu's newsstand— from the *Yodel* to, I guess, the *Daily Standard.*

Mr. Sewell cleared his throat, and the reporters all stopped to poise pencils to notepads.

"I was not the target," Mr. Sewell boomed, "of this dastardly act, an act born out of the violence that threatens to swamp this great country of ours, from the streets of Chicago to"— and here he winked at the reporters—" 'The Sidewalks of New York.'" (The reporters all chuckled here.) "No, the real target was the American way of life. America itself is under siege, attacked on all sides. By whom, you ask? By bootleggers, drowning this country in the depravity of alcohol. By gangsters, who'd rather smash and grab than earn an honest living. By the immigrants and anarchists who'd rather destroy our way of life than adapt to it."

Pencils scratched frantically. Even I could tell this was good copy.

"Now, I don't know which of these nefarious forces have conspired to do me harm. But I can't say I'm surprised. The voice of the righteous is always resented by the forces of darkness."

A smattering of applause here, from some of Mr. Sewell's guys in PRESS: *DAILY STANDARD* badges. Probably the same guys who'd laughed on cue.

Mr. Sewell held up his hands again, as if calming a roaring crowd. "But I do know that there's one man to keep this country on track and its enemies at bay. A man with grit. A man with character. A man with"— here it comes, I thought—"vision. That man," Mr. Sewell paused dramatically, as if the assembled were held in suspense, "is Herbert Hoover." Clapping again from the *Daily Standard* suck-ups, and this time even they looked embarrassed about it.

"And that's why the *Daily Standard* staunchly endorses Herbert Hoover for president! Read the paper tomorrow for our official endorsement and all week for election coverage! That's all for today. Thank you."

Mr. Sewell pushed the doors closed against the onslaught of flashbulbs and throwaway questions and locked it with a flourish.

"Well!" He smoothed over his already flawless hair as the servants scattered back to their posts. "I think I said everything that needed saying. What did you think, Mrs. O'Doyle? And, eh, you there." I tried to slink away. "Martha?"

What I thought was that he seemed to be in an awfully good mood for someone who'd almost gotten blown up.

Fortunately, Ma spoke first. "A powerful speech, Mr. Sewell."

"Yes, very, um, powerful." I nodded, my eyes trained on my mop.

"But, Mr. Sewell," Ma continued, "shall we get a man or two on the perimeter of the house? For security? That was a close call, to be sure, and after the threats you received last month . . ."

Mr. Sewell wasn't listening to a word Ma said. He was looking at me. "You don't sound convinced, Martha. Do you have a difference of opinion?"

I looked at Ma, who closed her eyes wearily, as if telepathically willing me to agree with him.

"As I've said, we are all a team here, and as a member of that team, I value frankness in all matters. Now, what do you have to say?"

"It's just . . ." I could see Ma's eyes fly open and widen. "It's just that I didn't think newspapers were supposed to say who should be president." I opened my eyes back at Ma, as if to say, "What, did you know that?"

"Ah, is that the issue? Or is it that you disagree with my endorsement?" Mr. Sewell took a step closer to me. "Could it be that your allegiance lies with your countryman, Mr. Al Smith?"

I said nothing, and in response to my silence, he guffawed. "I take it you did not read my paper this morning? For if you did, you would know you're throwing your hat in with a loser."

I lowered my eyes. My extra fourteen cents this week had all gone to the gangster film.

He took my silence as acquiescence. "So you'd vote for Al Smith, anyway? Turn over our country to the pope?"

Confusion shook me out of my silence. "What? No, to Mr. Smith, sir, he's not the pope."

"But he's a Catholic." Mr. Sewell pronounced it Cath-o-lick, and he poured suspicion on each syllable.

"Which makes the pope—de facto—as the head of him, the head of the rest of us."

"Well, I don't think that's true."

"And you'd let your Al open the saloons again,"—I didn't dare say that, in Brooklyn, none of them had ever closed—"and allow the blood of gang violence to come to our very front doors? And you'd see the pure, honest country lanes and village squares of this great country become, like your Mr. Smith revels in, 'the Sidewalks of New York?'"

I had many thoughts. Many things I'd like to say. But as I looked at Ma, I saw that we also had many bills to pay.

"No, sir, I guess not," I murmured, suddenly and assiduously swabbing my mop around the floor.

"You guess not, eh?" I could feel his eyes on the top of my head, looking down from on high. "Well, I *guess* it's a good thing you won't be voting. And thank God, as of tomorrow, I shan't be hearing that idiotic song about sidewalks again!" And he turned on his heel—leaving a black mark on the floor— returning to his office.

I couldn't help myself. "That's only if Hoover wins, sir."

"If?" He stopped and slowly turned back, regarding me like a simpleton. "*If* Hoover wins? Do you think I would allow any other outcome?"

"I don't see how it's up to you, sir. You're only allowed one vote."

He walked back over to me, bent over, and ruffled my hair. "No, dear," he said quietly, his hot breath smelling of black coffee, "*you* are only allowed one vote. I have one million, stretching from coast-to-coast, wherever the *Daily Standard* is found. And as long as I'm its publisher, every one of those votes will go to Hoover."

He stood up. "Mrs. O'Doyle?"

"Yes, sir." Ma's voice sounded weary, weighted with her disapproval of me.

"Could you see that the steps are cleared of that trash?"

"Of course, sir. I'll get someone—"

At that moment, I think Ma and I suddenly realized that someone had been missing throughout the whole episode. The one person who should have been working the door, who might have seen . . .

"Yes, ma'am?" Alphonse crept in like a fog behind us. "The front steps. I will see to it immediately."

Alphonse turned away to get whatever cleaner removed a bomb blast from marble. Mr. Sewell turned back to his office, his candidate assured and his chambermaid put in her place. And Ma turned away from me, her head shaking, as if a scolding was the height of wasted effort.

"I must check on Miss Rose," she muttered, pulling out her ring of keys as she headed to the stairs. "The blast surely startled her, and Lord knows what the aftermath will be of that. . . ." Her voice trailed off.

The hall floor waited silently for me, freshly smudged by Mr. Sewell's shoes.

Fortunately, the angrier I got, the harder I mopped.

I hated the way Mr. Sewell spoke to me. Like I was an ignorant maid. Like he knew more than me about the things that mattered.

I hated more that it was true.

Whatever was happening behind all the cold, closed lifeless doors in this house, he knew about it.

And maybe he's right. Maybe I don't know anything.

But there's one person in this house who knows everything.

Ma.

Chapter
11

"Does it seem strange to you that Mrs. Sewell never leaves her rooms?"

We were stopped at the corner of Park and Seventy-Second, the early evening well dark. The night had been stealing in a few minutes at a time, a day at a time, and now we found ourselves in this blackened sea of glowing streetlamps at a time when, just a few weeks prior, the kids would still have been playing stickball in the street.

Ma had her face deep in her purse, rifling for a peppermint. Chef had loaded the day's chicken stew with garlic, which always provoked Ma's dyspepsia. (The stew actually was quite tasty, despite having the word "cocoa" in its name.) "And what do you expect me to say to that, Dr. Freud?" she muttered as she stifled a burp. "Yes, I think it's the height of normalcy to barricade yourself in a room?"

"What I mean is, do you think she needs help of some kind?"

The light turned green, but Ma stayed put, letting her purse drop back to the end of her arm and turning back to look at me. A taxi stopped in anticipation, but she waved it away. "What help, pray tell, is she missing? She has New York's finest doctors on call, a nurse standing by twenty-four hours a day, and a house full of servants." She struggled to stifle a burp, interrupting her lecture. "Not to mention my near constant attention. The entire household is designed around keeping her out of a loony bin, where she'd be heaped in with the screwballs and ruffians and Georgie Riordans of the world."

Was that such a terrible thing? We rubbed elbows with Georgie Riordan every day (not to mention Crazy Lady Minchin and the speakeasies' stranger regulars), and no one seemed to think it was any great hardship for us.

The light turned red again, and Ma kept talking.

"Miss Rose has everything Mr. Sewell's money can buy." She coughed around a burp or a lump in her throat, I couldn't tell which. "And his love, obviously. And still she founders."

She stopped talking long enough for a bus to rattle by, the driver laying on his horn the whole way.

In the moment of relative quiet that followed. I ventured, "And her money, you mean."

"What's that?" The light had turned green, and Ma was already heading for the other side of the park.

I trotted after Ma. "You said everything Mr. Sewell's money could buy. And *her* money too, right? Isn't Mr. Sewell spending that as well?"

"There is no more 'her money.'" Ma sighed. "There's the house and its contents: the paintings, the library, a few other baubles. That's all that's left of her father's fortune. But Mr. Sewell spends down *his* fortune maintaining them, just to keep her happy." She stopped to struggle with another rising belch. "You know he could give two hoots for that house and those pictures. He'd be rid of them in a flat minute if he could."

"So why doesn't he? Sell them, I mean?"

"As I said, they make her happy, and her happiness is foremost in his mind." A loud burp finally escaped from Ma's pursed lips. Too relieved to look embarrassed, she sighed and started walking again. "But even if he wanted to, he couldn't. They're hers, legally."

Like that rising belch, a bubble of a thought rose in my mind.

"Ma, what would happen if Miss Ro—I mean Mrs. Sewell went well and truly . . . well, nuts? If she did go into an asylum? Then would Mr. Sewell maybe take ownership over her things? Like how Mrs. Phelan cashes Georgie's Saint Vincent de Paul Society checks?"

Ma stopped again and turned back to me with a look I hadn't seen since I borrowed her Sunday stockings to make mud grenades with the twins.

"I can't believe what I'm hearing!" We'd reached the entrance to the subway by now, and with a shake of her head, she broke off to race down its steps. But almost immediately she flew back up. "You talk of your employer as if he is some kind of a monster!" Now I could see she was more baffled than angry. "Like it's some kind of story from one of your detective rags! Well, you like spinning yarns? Here's the story for you. Mr. Sewell is no monster imprisoning a fair maiden; he's a knight. A knight who married a princess who was cursed, and now *she's* become the monster.

"Every day, he fights the good fight." Ma turned back down the stairs wearily. "For Rose. For all of us."

I followed meekly behind Ma, scolded . . . but unconvinced. I wasn't sure Mr. Sewell did want his wife to get better. And I was even less sure why Ma believed it so fervently.

An infuriatingly brief postcard from Daddo—"*Next stop: Dixie!*"—awaited us when we got home. Ma glanced at it, then tossed it on the table to be buried under the grocer's bill. The boys and I dug it back out, poring over the mysterious illustrations of children chased by alligators and studying the postmark for clues.

"Why'd he mail it from Penn Station if he's headed down South?" I wondered aloud.

"Probably dropped it off while switching trains," noted Ma as she filled the tub with steaming water for the twins' scrub. "Don't worry," she said brightly, "he'll be back before you know it." But her promise sounded hollow.

I took my own soak while Ma settled the boys. Too lazy to pour a bath of my own, I sat knees up in the tepid water, listening to her wrestle pajamas over wet heads, tell stories of pirates and mermaids, lead prayers, lay out uniforms for the next day. Soon she'd be out preparing the morning's porridge, sorting her own uniform out, reviewing the bills, scratching out grocery lists, and attending to whatever else it took to keep our family afloat.

She had reason to believe in her employer, I supposed, when that employer stood between us and the hardship and hungry bellies that lurked around Willoughby Street.

With my own wet head on the pillow that night, I felt ashamed. Not so much for my ideas, but for the pain they'd caused Ma. For all the pain I'd caused Ma. From the moment I walked in that Fifth Avenue address, I'd caused nothing but trouble for her and her employer, and my inevitable expulsion would mean not just another dressing-down, but possible the sacking of the whole O'Doyle family. So if Ma had to believe that Mr. Sewell was a knight in shining armor to keep working for him, well then, so did I.

The wind creaked and moaned outside. A drafty damp swirled in from the windows and snuck into the wrinkles in my quilt. Whether the chill of the room or the chill between us, something drew me to the warmth of Ma's bed, where Ma snored lightly— still ladylike, I thought—on her side.

Ten years and nothing had changed: Daddo on the road, me padding in my bare feet and burying any bad thoughts under Ma's snoring body. I slipped one foot, then two, under her covers, gingerly tucking them behind her nightgown-wrapped knees. Rather than bolt from the shock of my icy feet, Ma hugged her knees tighter around them.

But even the welcome warmth couldn't push

two competing thoughts out of my head: Was Mrs. Sewell a victim of some nefarious plan? Or was she a goonie bird to start, luring me to crazytown with her fantastical ideas?

Tossing and turning, I grabbed in desperation Ma's well-pawed copy of *Jane Eyre* on her bedside, hoping its many syllables would bore me to sleep.

I skimmed the book by the streetlamp streaming in the window, flipping past orphan whinings in search of the adventure (of which there was almost none).

There was romance, however. The romance between a lowly governess and her powerful, brooding employer, who has a secret: a mad wife in the attic. Whom he is too noble a man to leave, though he loves this governess so very, very much.

And that's when I understood why Ma returned to this book, over and over.

Ma wasn't in love with Daddo anymore. She was in love with Mr. Sewell.

Chapter 12

The mailbox handle at midnight was ice cold on my gloveless hand. The shock of it made me yank my hand back and look down at the letter I held.

In this letter to Daddo, I denounced Ma as an imposter. This woman who we thought we knew—the woman who made me not only return a piece of penny candy I stole, but spend my First Communion money on sweets for the Brooklyn Catholic Orphan Asylum. The woman who insisted on two layers of wool underwear from October to May. Who crossed the street wherever two men or more gathered, lest she overhear "rough language," who marched for Temperance and taught Sunday School. Yes, this woman was a liar, a cheat, a brazen hussy only pretending to be a saint.

It was an impassioned plea mixed with condemnation, worthy of any pulpit or court of law, and I ended asking Daddo to come back and take me and the twins on the road with him. I also added in a few ideas about a family act, which I still think would have played big down South.

As the streetlight fell on the letter, I realized I had no stamp . . . and no address. Where would I send it? Daddo could be anywhere south of the Mason-Dixon line, or if the right gig came up, on the vaudeville stages of Timbuktu.

I pulled my coat tight around my nightgown. In the quiet, in the cold, I suddenly felt so very alone. Just as Ma must have felt every night in that cold, empty bed.

So instead of denouncing Ma's name from the rooftops, I grew quiet. Over the following days I mopped and dusted while I eavesdropped and observed. Out of the corner of my supposedly downturned eye, I shuddered as Ma yessed and sirred and bowed her head through every interaction with the Great Archer Sewell. I saw now how her eyes shone when he called her name. How her lashes fluttered when he gazed down on her. And how her cheeks flushed when he gave her a compliment. She seemed less like a grown woman and more like the silly girls in school who talked to boys in whispery sighs.

But as I watched, I noticed, too, how steady the compliments came: "You are a marvel, Mrs. O'Doyle!" and "Another job well done, Mrs. O'Doyle!" and "How could we do it without you?" I saw how Mr. Sewell would touch her shoulder—just for a moment—as he spun flattering words, and how he'd lean down from his great height to murmur instructions, his breath fluttering the loose wisps of Ma's hair. Or how he'd plant his hand lightly, but firmly on her elbow, guiding her to his chosen destination.

Mr. Sewell knew exactly what he was doing, I deduced. This was no embellishment of Ma's overactive imagination, no playacting as Jane Eyre. He was deliberately drawing her down this path. He wanted Ma to fall in love with him.

And yet the idea of a passionate love affair was not just ridiculous, but logistically absurd. There was hardly a moment when Mr. Sewell or Ma wasn't working. And Mr. Sewell's late-night dinners were well-enough attended by debutantes and showgirls. Ma was beautiful in my eyes, but I couldn't see any millionaire pursuing a married, harried, mother-of-three housekeeper over Clara Bow.

So why? Why draw out Ma's affections?

This is what I was wondering a few days later as I returned to the gallery. Ma had sent me in with a rug beater, with the direction to undrape all the scattered settees and lounge chairs and knock the tar out of them. Or dust really. Clouds of it filled the gallery—so much that when Ma finally came in to check my handiwork, I heard the jingling of her giant ring of keys before even seeing her.

The keys.

The same keys that jingled as Ma climbed the stairs each day on the way to Rose's locked room.

But not locked from the inside, it finally dawned on me. Locked—and unlocked—from the outside.

By Ma.

"And what are you staring at, may I ask?" Ma ventured as I held my rug beater frozen in the air.

"Your keys," I whispered.

"Yes?" Ma looked swiftly down, and her face settled with relief to see them right where she guarded them, linked to her belt. "Yes, what about them?"

"Mrs. Sewell," I started. "Captive . . ."

"Of course she's captive. She's a captive of her own mind. And I'd think that you . . ." She stopped and followed my eyes, still trained on her key ring. "What—just what are you suggesting?" Ma sounded shocked. "That *I'm* the one who stands between Miss Rose and her liberty?"

I lowered my rug beater, now a feeble weapon in my hand. I said nothing. What was there to say?

Ma took in a deep breath, then let it out. The very action tinkled the keys a bit. "Let me tell you," she said slowly, "let me tell you what *freedom* looks like for Miss Rose. Last year it looked like knocking McCagg senseless with a paperweight so she could wander up and down Fifth Avenue in a nightgown, banging on car doors and ranting about a Greek goddess."

She must mean Proserpina. Now probably wasn't the time to tell Ma that was her Roman, not Greek, name.

"Or this spring, freedom for Rose looked like falling out a window someone'd been foolish enough to leave unlocked and breaking both her ankles."

Surely she was trying to escape, I thought. "But Ma—"

"Or climbing on the roof. Or riding dumbwaiters. Or setting fire to the kitchen. And somehow, everyone ends up reading all about it in the *Yodel.* So yes, I *am* the only thing between Miss Rose and freedom: the freedom to get herself killed. Or kill her caretakers. Or to humiliate herself on a grand scale and be remembered as a sideshow act, long after we—God willing—are able to restore her health." She stopped to catch her breath. "So then, is it such a sin to protect our beloved girl from this kind of freedom?"

Suddenly I wasn't so sure I had it all right.

Ma's voice softened. "Martha, nothing makes my heart break so as the sound of the key in that lock. But it's for her own good, don't you see? You'd no more give her free rein than you'd let a toddler cross Lexington Avenue.

"And besides," Ma continued, "Mr. Sewell firmly believes she won't need any of this one day, if we can just maintain a sense of consistency with her routines . . ." Her voice faded away, as if she didn't entirely believe it.

Mr. Sewell.

"But Mr. Sewell," I started uncertainly, "he's behind this. He's got to be! He wants you to believe—"

"Dear Lord in Heaven!" She rubbed her face in her hands, then lifted it to look at me. "Yes, dear, I've heard it all before. Miss Rose says her husband is imprisoning her, and I am, and McCagg is, and Alphonse, too. And the food is salty, and the pomegranates are rotten, and there's a minotaur in the basement." She sighed heavily. "I've heard it all before." She checked her watch. "And now it's time for me to hear it all again."

Ma turned on her heel and left me in that dust-settled room, where I saw the drape had slipped off the painted Proserpina again. I walked over to rehang it, stopping to look at the pomegranate that started it all. The goddess's hand settled into her chest, that fruit of knowledge both shown off and held back. For the first time, I looked up, looked deep into the goddess's pool blue eyes, which seemed to say, "I told you. I told you you didn't want to know."

Chapter 13

Now when Ma walked, I could no longer hear her neatly clicking footsteps, only the jingling of keys. My eyes glued to the pavement, I followed that sound from the subway to the house the next morning, looking up only when a six-piece marching band—the now weary oompahs of "The Sidewalks of New York"—drowned her out. "Vote for Al Smith!" said one side of the big bass drum, and when they turned the corner, I saw the other read "Give Me Liberty or Give Me Beer!"

I'd almost forgotten. It was Election Day.

The servants had gathered just outside the Sewells' front door to see the small parade, but when they saw Ma, they quickly scattered, not wanting to be caught loafing. Only Alphonse stayed, munching on an egg sandwich.

"Here's Hoover promising a chicken in every pot, and still, some men only want beer," Ma tsked.

"Perhaps they want both, ma'am," offered Alphonse.

Ma gave him her sternest look. "Mr. Dupont, what does Mr. Sewell say about eating on the job?"

Alphonse wrapped up the scraps in his handkerchief and shoved it in his pocket. "That it has no place in this house, ma'am."

"So then I shouldn't have to remind you," and she strode off to the back entrance, as if to note that, even four feet away from the front door, she still knew her place and the correct entrance to use.

"Now, I wasn't *in* the house," Alphonse muttered, pulling the parcel back out of his pocket. He stuffed the last bite in his mouth and turned to go back inside.

"Wait!" I blurted, and Alphonse slowly turned back to look at me. "The paintings."

I paused, hoping he'd jump in to fill the silence left in the wake of the oompah band. He didn't.

"I've been thinking . . . the paintings. The myth—Proserpina." He nodded encouragingly. "I mean . . . it's her, right? Mrs. Sewell?"

He smiled and made a flourish with his hand as if to say "That's it."

"But does that mean . . ." I shook off the question and began again. "That means she's being held . . . well, not captive. But yes, captive! Is that what the paintings are there for? To tell us?"

He nodded as he looked up and down the street. No more pomp or parades; just the usual New Yorkers with their own places to go now. "And who is holding her captive?" he finally said, looking at me meaningfully.

I didn't want to say it. But it had to be said out loud. Still, I couldn't meet his eye.

"Ma. But—"

He finished the thought for me. "But, in the story, was it not Pluto who stole Proserpina?"

"Well, yes, Pluto, I guess. Her husband."

"Her husband, yes," he said.

I looked over my shoulder. "Mr. Sewell," I whispered. But this time he shrugged.

I grabbed his arm. "So who do we tell? The police? Or no, we'll go to the newspaper! But not the *Daily Standard*, obviously, but the *Yodel*! Or—"

He took my hand calmly, firmly, and released its grip on his arm. "No, not we. Not me. There is nothing to do."

"Nothing?"

"Now you know. And it changes nothing."

"It changes everything! It changes nothing only if you *do* nothing!"

"No. It changes nothing because the facts have not changed. The lady is mad. She stays in her room. Her husband wants her there. Trust me. Calling an alarm will not change a thing in the house, except perhaps your place in it."

"But," I sputtered, "but—but she isn't mad!" And yet as I said it, I realized, I didn't know. "At least, she wasn't! I mean, maybe she wasn't mad before! Or maybe she was," I mumbled, "but maybe she wasn't but she was driven mad by being locked away?"

"But don't you see? It is all the same. Mr. Sewell is a powerful man. He makes the story. And if he says his wife is mad, that is the end of it. She is." He brushed his hands together.

"Fine, if you won't help me, I'll tell—"

"Who? McCagg, her"—he laughed, not kindly— "'nurse'? He is the very man placed to keep her from escaping." And now his broad shoulders, his hamhock arms, his sleeping spot outside her room made sense. He wasn't there to step in when help was needed, but to keep help at bay.

"Chef? Magdalena?" Alphonse continued. "None

of the staff will lift a finger if they think they might lose their jobs. Bridie? Well, yes," he chuckled, "perhaps Bridie truly does not know. I think she still believes in fairies also. Your mother—"

He thought for a while, looking down the street and fiddling with the baby mustache that was sprouting on his lip.

"Somehow," he said as he turned finally to go back inside, "Mr. Sewell has convinced your mother that this bizarre scene is in service to her mistress. So let us just say, the lady of the house is not the only one that Mr. Sewell has imprisoned."

Chapter
14

The next day the bands and buttons and stumpers had disappeared, replaced by tired, deflated people pulling their coat lapels together as they trudged to work or to their local speak. Hoover had won. Their mayor had failed; America was still the heartland, and New York was still an island.

And Mr. Sewell was right: His story counted more than any other.

Especially in this house.

So according to him, Rose was mad. Mad enough to lock herself away. But that I knew wasn't true, whatever he claimed. *He* was locking her away. But was he hiding away Rose because of her madness? Or was he driving her mad by hiding her away?

It was a chicken-egg scenario which made a crazy omelette, however you scrambled it.

A few days later I was dusting in one of the front parlors where, judging from the number of cigarette lighters and an untouched bar cart, the Pritchards had once entertained afternoon callers. On one of the bookshelves flanking the fireplace, I came across a row of scrapbooks. Mrs. Sewell must have kept them back when she was Miss Rose and enamored of her press coverage. I pulled one off the shelf; it was stuffed with clippings from every newspaper in the city and not a few abroad.

NEW TO THE SOCIETY SET:
Introducing Miss Rose Pritchard of Charleston, West Virginia

BY INVITATION ONLY:
Extraordinary Art Collection Hosted Today by Miss Rose Pritchard

DEBUT WITHOUT A DEBUTANTE:
Miss Pritchard Trades Own Party for Cabaret Spotlight

PRAY FOR A BREEZE, BOYS! . . .
Another Hemline Gasper from Rose Pritchard!

MONEY CAN'T BUY CLASS:
Another Shameful Display by Miss Rose Pritchard

PRICELESS "PICASSO" SOLD AT AUCTION REVEALED TO BE PRODUCT OF ROSE PRITCHARD'S FEET!

OUR HERO!: MISS ROSE PRITCHARD
"Luxe Lemonade Stand" Said to Have Raised "Thousands" for War Effort

RAILROAD HEIRESS JOINS UNION PICKET LINES AGAINST OWN FATHER'S FACTORY

OUR ROSE TRADES NEWPORT SEASON FOR TOUR BY CARGO SHIP
Packing List: "Rouge and a Rucksack"
Sightings Rumored in Marrakech, Bombay, Shanghai

"WILD ROSE"—OR ROTTEN ONE?
Why Today's Generation Is Mad, Bad, and Dangerous to Know

MISS PRITCHARD ENGAGED AT LAST!
Wedding of the Year Predicted
Newspaper Scion Announced to Be Heiress's Choice (Good Luck, Archie!)

That's where the clippings ended.

And they did nothing to clear up any questions. In fact, Rose was like one of those headshrinker tests—the kind where what you saw said more about you than her.

Depending on the paper or the writer or even the day, Rose could be called wild, wise, bold, spoiled, modern, brazen, thrilling, or treacherous. And she didn't seem to care what you called her. From what she'd pasted in that scrapbook, she relished condemnation and celebration equally.

To this day, Mr. Sewell said she was ill, unmanageable, possibly dangerous.

Ma said whatever Mr. Sewell said.

The doctor said she was hysterical, unfeminine, just needed rest.

And Alphonse said as little as possible.

There was only one way to figure her out. I had to see the Wild Rose for myself.

A squeaking escaped from the butler's pantry down the hall: the sound of Mrs. Sewell's breakfast tray being sent down to the kitchen via the dumbwaiter to be cleared and traded for lunch. Another door to the dumbwaiter lay hidden here on the first floor, in this small room where a butler and team of footman once removed some other chef's platters and trays and delivered them across the hall, still steaming hot, to a dining room full of socialites and dignitaries.

No visitors were expected today—at least, not until Mr. Sewell's latest late-night fire drill. In fact, it was almost time for the servants to head down to the basement dining hall for their own midday meal. For the next hour, everyone would be at lunch.

Well, almost everyone. McCagg was never invited to this luncheon. He remained at his hall post, with a lunch tray Ma brought up ahead of time.

I tiptoed over to the small room. Opened the door to the dumbwaiter. Peeked down the shaft, where Mrs. Sewell's breakfast plates rattled as they made their rough landing. Another small door downstairs clicked open, Bridie's capable hands clearing the leftovers out, preparing to load the next cargo in.

I had an idea.

"Bridie, my girl," I said a little too brightly, "what's that delicious smell?"

"Well, hello, Martha!" Her face was open and guileless, illuminated by the one ray of sunshine that struggled in through the street-level window. "How do you like this lunch tray, I wonder?"

Where I had usually smushed some butter on scraped-off toast, Bridie had arranged golden triangles of buttery goodness on a pretty Wedgwood plate.

"There's three different kinds of preserves—the gooseberry is my own Gran's recipe!—and I thought, with doctor's permission, she might like a soft-cooked egg."

Chef nodded approvingly at Bridie and then pointedly at me. I scowled back. No one ever solved a mystery with soft-cooked eggs.

"Well, Mrs. Sewell is lucky to get it," I said, backing away to the door as Bridie lifted the tray into the dumbwaiter.

I heard the click of the dumbwaiter door as I sprinted up the back stairs to the ground floor, rounding the corner to the butler's pantry. With a last look over my shoulder, I opened the square-shaped door, just in time to see Bridie's lunch tray rise into view. As soon as the rising box lined up with the door frame, I pushed hard down on the box, causing it to stop momentarily, and climbed in, pulling the door just to—but not closed—behind me.

I heard Bridie's voice through the shaft below. "It's stuck. Chef, the dumbwaiter's stuck!" Then the box jerked upward, Chef's brawny, Cordon Bleu–trained arms surely giving the pulley rope a strong tug.

I rose and rose, held tight in that moving coffin, until I came to a jerky stop. A small bell rang with my stop to alert the mistress of her delivery.

Curled up, my knees to my nose, I waited.

I felt my bum sink into the gooseberry jam. I waited some more.

Just as I began to wonder how much oxygen you got in a standard dumbwaiter, I heard heavy breathing on the other side of the door.

Finally, with a click, it opened.

I had thought she might scream and was ready to jump out and put my hand over her mouth if necessary. But Mrs. Sewell only looked at me hazily, unsteady on her feet, her long loose hair and blotchy face mussed with too much sleep.

After a minute of staring, she licked her dry lips and said thickly: "The pomegranate."

"Yes. That was me." By instinct, I spoke slowly. Made no sudden movements. "A pomegranate for . . . Proserpina?"

She nodded to herself and staggered to a nearby chair, settling herself with a thud.

Despite her fancy, lacy nightgown, and despite being only in her thirties by my calculations, she looked like the old rag woman who sometimes drank rum and fell asleep on our stoop. She was thin, drawn, with gray skin, a stark contrast to the paintings that hung from every corner of the room, with their fat goddesses and radiant pink-cheeked cupids.

I immediately felt terrible about sitting on her lunch. "Here, Mrs. Sewell," I jumped out and peeled the slices of toast off my skirts, "eat. You look peaked."

"It's Rose," she muttered, more to herself than to me. "Not Mrs. Sewell. Never Mrs. Sewell. Never Mrs. Sewell." At the sight of the squashed toast, she closed her eyes and groaned slightly, then peered at me through squinty lids. "Is there tea?"

I went back to the dumbwaiter and found the teapot, luckily still upright, and poured her out a cup with milk. She took it, sighing to embrace the warmth in her hands, and took a sip.

"Salty," she sighed.

I'd seen Bridie add the sugar myself.

I wasn't quite sure where to begin. Are you all right? Are you being mistreated? Do you want to escape?

And how do you ask: Are you crazy?

But, looking at the staggering, muttering heap in the armchair, I wasn't sure I needed to anymore.

"Look, Mrs. Sewell, I mean Rose—" As I moved swiftly to crouch at her feet, I triggered a bundle of paintings leaning against the wall. The whole lot tipped over like dominoes, a half-dozen frames clattering to the floor.

"Mizzus Sewell?" came a gravelly voice just outside the door.

McCagg.

"Mizzus, what you up to in there?" The squeak of a chair pushed back by a large man's backside rang out. A ring of keys jangled.

For the first time, I saw alarm—no, fear—in Rose's dead eyes. "Go!" she hissed, pushing me toward the dumbwaiter with what little strength her bony arms had.

I ran to the square door, stuffing myself inside and closing myself in, as I heard McCagg open up the room.

"What's the fuss this time? Toast not the right shade of brown?" I heard him grumble.

But that was all I heard, because the opening and closing of the dumbwaiter door had set off a bell in the kitchen, and Bridie, assuming her mistress had loaded her dirty dishes, began to work at the pulley again, and I descended.

When I emerged from the butler's pantry, it wasn't long before I found Ma hunting for me, annoyed by my abandoned carpet sweeper in the parlor. I dutifully returned to working the Bissell over the carpet by longitude and latitude.

There was no one to rescue, I stewed with disappointment, no adventure to be had. There was just a loony woman in the attic, an embarrassment to her big-shot husband, who could lock her up and garner no more than a shrug from the servants just grateful to have a job. And just one day after another, polishing a lifeless tomb.

But later that afternoon, I saw Ma gesture to Alphonse, and after conferring for a few moments, Ma flung open the gallery doors for him.

"Miss Rose has started up again," Ma said with a sigh as Alphonse carried the four paintings, one by one, up the stairs and back to Rose's room. And brought one back down, wrapped again in a sheet.

Once he was done hanging it, he left, refusing to meet my eye. Ma closed the doors behind him.

Proserpina was just the beginning of the story, I thought. And now she's sent down the next chapter.

Chapter 15

I had the doors open before Ma's feet hit the last step on the servants' stairs.

And I heard Alphonse's footsteps behind me before I could set a foot in.

He helped me pull back the sheet, and he whistled to see it again.

"A Rembrandt, this one," he said, stepping back for a better view. "It is outside belief the collection she has up there. Like locking the Louvre in an attic."

Eh, I thought. I didn't like this one so much.

A rich lady with flushed cheeks and a double chin leaned with one hand braced against a table. Her other hand lay at the bottom of her rib cage in what I guessed was a graceful gesture but looked more like a heartburn attack. Her stance seemed heavy, but her face was serene, and given the posh velvets and pearls that surrounded her, I wasn't surprised. Like the still lifes she'd replaced, she summoned you to peep at her wealth: shiny paisley silks, furs around her shoulders. A young girl, a maid, I supposed, brought her a drink in a bejeweled seashell.

Sophonisba, the plaque on the frame read. "Who the—?" I asked aloud.

"Sophonisba, a queen of Carthage. She lived during the Second Punic War—"

"Are you a teacher or something?" I couldn't help but break in. "How do you *know* all this anyway?"

Alphonse looked taken aback. I was beginning to see that while he'd gladly natter about art, books, mythology, even his employers, his own story was one to be approached delicately. He walked away from the painting, pacing a bit in the echoing gallery, considering something. Finally he responded, "Yes, I was a teacher, in my old country," as if he were confiding something of great importance and discretion, and I burst out laughing at his somber expression.

"Is that so hard to believe?" He seemed hurt and set about tidying up his suit, as if his footman's uniform were to blame.

"Not at all," I chuckled. "It explains everything." It explained what a scolding know-it-all he was and why I always felt as if he were going to chide me for not finishing my reading.

"I taught in a school, Greek and Latin. I taught boys like you."

"I'm not a boy," I retorted.

"No, that is true. Girls do not study Greek or Latin. But you are like them. You want only for me to give you the answers, do none of the study yourself."

"Girls can so study Greek and Latin!" I flashed.

"I did not say that they couldn't." He bowed slightly. "I say that, as a rule, they do not." And he smiled, waiting for me to disprove him.

"So what happened?" I sidestepped. "How did you end up here?"

He paused again before speaking. "My parents had a café. They made—how do you say—*pasticcini?*"

"Pasta? Like noodles?"

"No, like *cannoli*—"

"Oh, pastry!"

"Yes," he pointed at me lightly, "this is it. We would work in the shop with them, my older brother and I. Long, long hours. Seven days a week, only an afternoon off every two Sundays.

"My brother and I hated this work. We loved books. He says, okay, he will help with the shop if I can go to school. And then he will go to school next. So that is what we did: I went to school with my fingers in books, and he stayed with his fingers in the pastry. I studied Greek, Latin, even English." He cleared his throat. "Also Italian. I speak some Italian.

"I started teaching. This, I love. Even with the students who were not so good; when I would share these stories," and here he gestured to the painting, "I would see their eyes . . . how do you say? Lighten? Light up? How incredible, I thought. To share the same stories that speak to the imagination for thousands of years, right here, today."

"But why aren't you a teacher anymore?"

"My brother also had dreams. He wanted a new life in America. When my mother died, he cannot bear to stay any longer. He worked so many years for me. So I came with him."

"No," I said frustrated. "Why aren't you a teacher here?"

Alphonse shook his head. "You Americans—you are more interested in making new stories than hearing the old stories. Not so much interested in the classics, and not so many teacher jobs for foreigners." He flapped the lapels of his footman uniform again. "But always many jobs for servants. It is the land of opportunity, after all. For some," and he looked around the room, with its silk wallpaper and ceiling like a cathedral. And back to the lady in the painting, with her own display of luxury.

"And what new life did your brother discover in America?" I asked.

He seemed to return to himself, assuming a businesslike manner. "None at all," he said. "He's dead."

I flushed. "Oh, I'm sorry."

"Now this painting." He moved on. "Sophonisba. A great woman hero of Roman literature—Petrarch? Yes, Petrarch. But the cup . . . perhaps this is why Mrs. Sewell chose it."

I looked at the painting again. At the young maid bringing her mistress that drink. Perhaps a nice hot cup of tea, just as I had brought Rose this morning.

"Oh," Alphonse reached into his jacket pocket, "also. When I get the painting," he said, "the lady also give me this book. To return downstairs." But instead of returning it to the library, he handed it to me: a small leather-bound volume, with gilt-edged pages. I opened it to the first page, which read: *Great Heroines of Antiquity.*

For the rest of the day, I sneaked looks between making tracks with the carpet sweeper. Waiting for Ma to pass from room to room, I hid behind sofas

I was supposed to be plumping and paged through the chapters with dusty fingers.

Sophonisba . . . well, quite honestly, I couldn't make heads or tails of it. First she married one fellow, then some other one. One or another got defeated by the Romans in a war. The Romans wanted to parade Sophonisba around like some kind of victory trophy, and her husband said death would be preferable to this (which I guess was easy for him to say). So he sent her a cup of poison, and she drank it.

I scuttled back to the gallery like a mouse, staying close to the walls.

The drape was still off, forgotten on the floor. And on the canvas, the young maid still had her back to me, as she offered the seashell cup of poison to her mistress, sent by the husband.

Her husband sent a cup of poison. Her maid gave it to her. She drank it.

I pictured Rose again from this morning. Pale. Unsteady. Blotchy. Not well.

Could she really believe her husband was poisoning her? And that her servants—even me?—were the messengers?

If this is what Rose suspected, I thought with a shiver down my spine, then she was either crazier than I thought . . . or in more danger than I could imagine.

It didn't take me long to suspect just what mysterious substance was in that cup.

And it didn't take much to distract Bridie with a concocted task or to wait for Chef to sneak into the pantry for a nip of cooking wine.

I ruled out Mrs. Sewell's tea quickly enough—its packaging was fancier than necessary, to be sure, but its smell and its small, flaky, black leaves were like any tea I'd ever seen.

Then there was that *special sugar*, secured by Mr. Sewell from some exotic location. A sugar that, when I put a bit on my tongue, actually tasted salty, just as Mrs. Sewell said, with a slightly metallic aftertaste.

This couldn't be some juvenile trick of Mr. Sewell's, I thought, the way I used to put sugar in the salt cellar for April Fools'. Surely there was something in this salty-sugar or sugary-salt that was poisoning Rose.

I tied a spoonful in my handkerchief. There was only one way to find out.

Chapter
16

I trotted out my woman troubles story on Ma and headed back to Brooklyn early, willing the subway on to reach home before five o'clock, when Mr. Phelan closed his pharmacy. His was our local, the site of Sunday afternoons at the soda counter and late night knocks on his upstairs apartment door for fever reducers. But as my hand wrapped around the doorknob, and I glanced the back of his balding head through the window, I could already picture his skeptical, gossiping face. Whatever we discussed would be in Ma's ear by nightfall.

So without the door giving so much as a jingle, I walked on.

The thing I love about Brooklyn is that you can cross countries and even continents, if you just keep walking long enough. So I kept walking deeper into Brooklyn, past signs for Flanagan's Five and Dime ("Everything under the sun!") and Gallagher's Hardware ("Where your 'to-do' list gets done!"), past Gottschalk Household Goods ("It's got to be Gottschalk!"), and Shapiro & Sons Fine Dresses ("If you can find a better price, your brother must be in the business!"), past butcher shops with names devoid of vowels and slogans. I stopped at a few shops with the telltale red cross hanging over their doors, but they were either closed or the babble of languages at the counter drove me back outside.

I kept walking until I reached Bedford Avenue.

Across Bedford was off-limits. Across Bedford was where "the other kind" lived, as Ma put it, and you didn't want to go there alone.

But then, Ma was wrong about a lot of things, I was starting to think.

Here I was relieved to hear only English in the streets, but the voices had a different cadence—swingier, janglier, with broad English accents here and there—and people came in all shades, from almost as light as my "white Irish glow" to an astounding shade of blue-black. I held myself upright, on guard for the unnamed danger Ma always warned about, but no one gave me any notice. Other whites wandered freely, shopping, even socializing with the men and women on the sidewalks, and I wondered: Did they not know about the unnamed danger . . . or did they believe Ma was wrong, too?

When I saw the next red cross hanging over a lane, I turned and entered the shop underneath, relieved to escape the threat of a threat.

The shop resembled Mr. Phelan's in almost every way: a small soda counter and baubles up front, brightly colored boxes and bottles lining the walls, more mysterious potions behind the counter. The same mothers wiping kids with snotty noses, the same constipated-looking old biddies, the same shifty men in line with prescriptions for "medicinal" alcohol. I let out a small sigh of recognition.

I compared the brands of hair tonic in too much detail until the bulk of the customers had cleared out.

"I know what you're looking for," called out a soft voice, deep and royal with something like the King's English.

I turned cautiously, hoping he was speaking to another customer. But I was the only one left.

"I keep them here, behind the counter," said the man. His grizzled hair matched the white coat he wore over a natty suit, a camel color that seemed a natural outgrowth from his deep brown skin. As I drew closer, I was surprised to notice he had freckles like me. "Girls like you were stealing them, too embarrassed to ask."

He pushed an enormous box labeled Kotex across the counter to me. "It's nothing to be ashamed of, girl," he clucked quietly. "It's as natural as the tides."

My own freckles must have flared as my face turned red. "No, I'm not—I mean, that's not why I'm—" I fumbled in my pocket for the handkerchief I'd knotted back at Bridie's workstation. "Here," I said, holding it out, "it's this."

He looked at my hand for a moment, then plucked up the handkerchief gingerly between his thumb and forefinger.

"And this is . . .?" He left the thought unfinished.

"No, nothing . . . unpleasant." My mind scrambled for some plausible story. "My ma, uh, found a bottle in the kitchen. Unmarked, you see, with this . . . powder in it. She's not sure if it's sugar, or salt, or um, medicinal in nature. Maybe you could say?" He looked at me strangely. "She hates to throw it out if it's useful," I hastened to add.

"Ah." The pharmacist continued to weigh me with his eyes. "And naturally, she sent you here?" He cocked his head, taking in my cheeks, still pink, and my hair which had never seemed more red than in that moment.

"Well," I said, trying to sound assured and sophisticated, "I was passing through."

He chuckled to himself. "Yes. Passing through. Of course." He weighed the handkerchief in his palm, bouncing it up and down slightly, while still considering me.

Finally he set it on the counter and went to work on the knot.

"Well, let's see what you've brought me, Miss . . .?"

"Oh. It's Marth—Marguerite," I blurted.

More slow nodding. "Marguerite, it is? Well," he reached over the counter to shake my hand, "how do you do? I am Dr. Murphy."

"Murphy?" I responded without thinking, "Oh, we have a whole Murphy clan on our block. Jack Murphy, John Murphy, Sean Murphy, the other Sean Murphy—" I stopped when I realized there wasn't likely any relation.

He smiled indulgently. "No, I don't know them. I think we are from different parts of the isles." He opened the handkerchief flat on the counter. "My Irish heritage comes by way of Jamaica."

I'd never met a black Irishman, but then, I'd never crossed Flatbush before either.

The doctor manipulated the handkerchief a bit, watching the crystals of the powder shift and glimmer in the electric light that hung over the counter. Then he licked his pinkie, dipped it into the powder, and he touched it to the tip of his tongue. Like me, I saw him screw up his face a little.

"Salty in taste."

"Yes, exactly!" I jumped in. He gave me that suspicious look again, and I shut up.

"That indicates a sodium base. Could be one of several varieties though." The door opened, letting in a neatly kept grandmother whose complaints could only be suggested in the broadest of terms. I moved back to the hair tonic until the pharmacist was able to decode and prescribe the right remedy. Once she left, he waved me back over. "Wait here," he said, and went into the back room.

He came back with a small glass test tube in its holder, a pitcher of water, and a small bottle marked silver nitrate.

"You know this from chemistry class, yes?"

I shrugged. "I'm a girl. I don't think we take chemistry."

"That is the silliest thing you've said since you told me your name is Marguerite."

I said nothing in return to that.

He dropped a pinch of the powder into the test tube. "Now," he said, pouring a slug of water into the tube as well, "when you add a few drops of silver nitrate, the ions recombine, and what's left behind is a precipitate."

"A what?"

"Residue. Let's say, stuff," he said, swirling the tube until the crystals disappeared, absorbed into the water. He reached for the other bottle and picked up its dropper, then squeezed off a few drops of the substance into the test tube.

"That is our magic, right there." And like a real magician, he obscured the test tube with his hand, roiling it around and around in the air, its transformation hidden behind his palm. "If it is sodium chloride—simple table salt to you and me—we'll see a clean white residue left behind.

"Sodium fluoride, on the other hand," and here he actually switched the tube to his left, still concealing its magic, "would leave behind nothing, as sodium fluoride is soluble." He looked at my blank face. "It dissolves." He peeked at the tube. "Is anyone in the family having tooth trouble?"

I thought back to my conversation with Rose. She hadn't had much opportunity to smile. But her teeth seemed strong and white, the teeth of a rich girl. I shook my head.

"Then there's sodium iodide." The tube swirled its way back to his right hand. "There we'll see a pale yellow precipitate." This time he looked at me instead of the tube. "You're a skinny girl, aren't you? Quick, too."

"I suppose."

"How do you like fish?"

I shrugged. "It's all right. I love oysters, though! I can slurp down a dozen, raw. More if my dad dares me!" Then I shut my trap again, because I was supposed to be thinking about Rose's symptoms, not mine. I wasn't sure whether fish was on her menu of bland.

He peeked again at the tube, then began to get the test tube stand ready. "That brings us to sodium bromide. In which we'd see a cloudy white residue. Something like a thickened cream."

Finally he held the tube up to the light.

The liquid in the test tube spun like its own tornado, then calmed, a cloudy cluster of white settling to the bottom.

We both stared at it for a minute. Then Dr. Murphy put the tube softly into the test tube holder.

"Sodium bromide," he began sternly, "is a strong treatment. It should *never* be left out, may God forbid, unlabeled. Should you mistake this for common table salt, the results could be dire."

"Dire," I whispered. "Sir?"

"Bromides have a long half-life." He saw the confusion on my face and continued. "They don't flush out of the system easily; they can stay in the blood for a long time, building up."

I nodded thoughtfully, but he could see that I still didn't get it.

"Yes, they may soothe symptoms at the beginning, but the more you use them, the more toxic they become. In low doses, side effects may be headaches, stomach discomfort with attending loss of appetite, along with the expected somnolence"— he paused—"*sleepiness,* even lethargy. But in higher doses one might see restlessness, irritability, confusion, disorientation, even hallucinations. And on the skin sometimes—"

"Rashes," I whispered.

He narrowed his eyes. "Yes," he consented, and I saw his gaze pass over my clear face, neck, and arms.

"And—death?" I gasped.

The doctor frowned this time. "No," he said carefully. "At least—unlikely, at this dosage."

"So it wouldn't kill you. But it would make you seem crazy?"

"Yes. Still, it's likely too strong a treatment—"

"But—what is it a treatment *for*?"

"There are much safer sedatives, if that is needed." He pushed aside the test tube, and leaned a bit closer. His voice became kind rather than stern. "At home, is everything—"

"What's a sedative?"

He spoke even more slowly, with more concern now, as if his own ponderous voice could slow my rapidly beating heart. "For nervous conditions. For calming nervousness, anxiety—"

"Wild, strange behavior?"

"Yes," he assented.

"So you're saying," I worked it out slowly, "you might take these—"

"Bromides," he prompted.

"Bromides," I acknowledged, "if you're crazy." I thought, and then said, "Wild. But if you take too much—or if someone gives you too much—they might make you crazier?"

"Yes, that is one way to put it." He thought for a moment, then reaffirmed, "Yes. I'm afraid so. Extended use could cause greater mental distress than any original symptoms."

And I remembered—for the first time—that outburst, quite literally that burst of energy and life, came the day after I'd forgotten to add the "sugar" to her porridge.

"And if you stopped taking them all of a sudden—"

"Yes, I would recommend that—"

"—would you get," I fished around for the right word, "squirrelly?"

He gave me that strange look again. Finally he said, "Yes. You might become very . . . distressed. But," he said firmly, "it is the only way."

Who was to blame, my mind set off, for Rose's high doses? Had the doctor written the high prescriptions? He would know the dosage was too high. Or was Mr. Sewell sneaking it in, without the doctor's knowledge? My mind went back to the jar in the kitchen, which Mr. Sewell kept stocked with the "fancy sugar" he said Rose insisted on. *He* insisted on, I could see now. Maybe at first to make her more "manageable." But then for the way it made Rose seem progressively more and more insane. Not wild or madcap or eccentric, but genuinely crazy.

These were Rose's pomegranate seeds, I realized: the food that kept her trapped in her upstairs version of the underworld.

Dr. Murphy's voice interrupted my wild wonderings.

"Listen, Miss Marguerite, I know you may not be from"—he looked outside, where a group of boys were horsing around in the dusk—"around here. But if you have trouble with anything—with your family, with your household, what have you—you come back here. Or bring your ma or your pa or whoever it is that troubles you. It doesn't matter where you are from. You understand?"

I nodded.

"We Irish have to stick together, right?" He winked.

I laughed in spite of myself. "Yes, I guess we do."

"Now, you tell your ma what I told you. And if it's all right with you, I think I might throw the rest of this away."

"Yes, Dr. Murphy. Please do. We won't miss it."

The next day, while Bridie was in the loo, I washed the "special sugar" down the slop sink and replaced it with plain old white sugar from the pantry.

And I waited for all hell to break loose.

Chapter 17

What settled over the house was more frightening than a series of rages and outbursts.

It was a fevered, hushed silence.

Once in the park, in the spring, my brothers were hunting for worms for fishing when they came across a small brown cylinder. They broke it open, hoping for an avalanche of those fluffy white seeds that float on the wind, but recoiled to find the fully formed, decomposing carcass of a butterfly. Its wings had been a yellow-orange meant to glimmer in the sunlight, but black rot had begun to eat away at the edges, and its fuzzy body, sheltered under its folded wings, had gone soft. The boys threw it to the ground and dared each other to touch it until they found a frog to chase, but I dug a little grave for it and said a Hail Mary. There was something unbearably sad in that cocoon, the idea that the doomed creature had been ready to be born, but died fighting for release.

For the next few weeks, I couldn't stop thinking about that butterfly.

Ma raced up and down the stairs with towels and thermometers and vials, and the dumbwaiter was kept busy with bowls of broth and a collection of empty pots, which came back covered with the wet and dirty towels.

"I'm afraid we should call in Dr. Westbrook again," I overheard her saying early on to Mr. Sewell in the hallway. She had caught him as Alphonse helped him on with his overcoat, cold air blustering through the front doors where his new silver Duesenberg idled out front.

"Good idea, good to get his opinion," Sewell intoned, putting on his hat and grabbing a silver-topped cane that, I thought, made him look like Mr. Peanut. "She's worse, you think?" he said, and I thought I heard a bit of hope in his voice.

"She's fevered and uncomfortable," she said, squeezing her hands together as if she were praying. "And unable to keep anything down. Maybe Dr. Westbrook has a draft of something that could help settle her—"

"No!" I shouted from my spot in the front parlor, where I'd been half polishing one doorknob. All three in the foyer turned to stare at me.

"I don't care for servants eavesdropping," Mr. Sewell flashed to my mother. (This struck me as quite funny, as that is all that servants do.)

Ma glared at me, but I couldn't chance the doctor prescribing bromides again and derailing the process of clearing out Rose's system. I jumped in before she could chide me. "Ma, don't you always say to sweat a fever? 'The fire that purifies,' you say. You don't want to stop the body doing its natural work, now do you?"

Ma pursed her lips and finally assented. "That is true. It's what I'd do for my own children."

Mr. Sewell looked annoyed. I knew he hoped to get the doctor in to show off how "sick" Rose was, to continue to build his case for her incapacity. But he still needed Ma on his side, for her to think he thought the world of her.

"Then it's settled," he said reluctantly. "But keep an eye over it, Mrs. O'Doyle, and don't hesitate to call Dr. Westbrook if you think she takes a turn!"

As he turned to go, I couldn't help but think he stopped to regard me a split second longer than a man like him should regard a parlormaid. Which is to say, a split second at all.

With Rose under her care, Ma was distracted and left more of the work to our discretion. This did nothing to inspire more rigor in my work.

Instead, I spent my energies on plotting Mrs. Sewell's escape, once she was well and clear of the poisons clouding her system.

You might wonder why I didn't go straight to the police. That's what they do in movies, and it's the first thing they teach you at school: If you're lost, find a policeman.

First of all, one couldn't help but notice that our block had more cops than you could shake a stick at: reserving an unofficial parking spot for Mr. Sewell's Duesenberg, moving along any riffraff, working a beat that seemed to consist of this block and this block only. Something told me that Mr. Sewell gave gladly and generously to the Patrolmen's Benevolent Association.

Second of all, there was the kidnapping.

Last year, I'd had a fight with Ma over my plan to join an overnight campout at Breezy Point. A kid from the neighborhood had an aunt with a summer cottage there, and we were all going out on a Friday night to swim and fish and build a bonfire and sleep under the stars. Sheila Morrison said she'd say I was staying at her house, but then a particularly affecting homily by Father Riordan had her examining her conscience and confessing all to her mother, including some past capers of ours that really could have stayed buried.

The neighborhood party line ensured Ma knew everything, and she vowed she'd lock me in my room if she had to. But then Mr. Sewell had one of his late visitors that Friday night which required Ma's attention, and when she wasn't home by supper, I parked the boys at Mrs. Annunziata's and headed to the A train.

I stayed at the shore all weekend, even though it poured a cold, sodden rain as if it were winter in Belfast. Eventually, the girls drifted home in twos, bored by the boys' efforts to make their own gin and impress us with their poor wrestling skills.

On the train home on Sunday, my stomach churned to think of the lashing I'd get—for lying, for abandoning the twins, for ruining my mother's one day off, for making her "sick with worry," the most common illness up and down the streets of

Brooklyn, it seemed. I feared less the punishment than the row that I knew would go into the night, and the leaden guilt that would stay with me for days, maybe weeks, afterward.

I was walking from the train in a dark downpour when I passed the local police precinct. And my feet seemed to just carry me inside, to that dry, well-lighted hall, where the red-haired cops were all familiar faces from Daddo's haunts. Before I knew it, I had a blanket thrown around me, a mug of tea in my hands, and a tale spilled out that impressed even me with its lurid details and scope, a tale of chloroform-wielding kidnappers and rope and dank basements and a mysterious woman mastermind named "Mexicali Rose."

The station went into an uproar; phone calls were made, and wires were sent. When I heard the examination room door open, I was sure it would be a journalist from the *New York Times*, but my stomach dropped to see a frowning Ma. In the end, I wasn't helped by the fact that I'd lifted most of the details of my story from something I'd read in the tabloids, a lady preacher from California who'd pulled the same stunt.

So any credibility I would ever have with the New York Police Department had been destroyed. For life.

In the rescue of Rose, I'd get no help from New York's Finest. So I examined doorways and windows, looking for an exit that might go unnoticed. Once, when McCagg was in the washroom, I tried quickly to pick the lock to Rose's room as I'd seen Declan Leary do once, but Mr. Sewell had invested in some kind of lock that already knew the tricks of a girl's hairpin. I looked for opportunities to steal Ma's keys, thinking that if I could get a copy made of the key to Rose's room, I could let her out myself. If I distracted McCagg. And Ma, and all the rest of the household staff. And Mr. Sewell.

It drove me crazy, when I took my quick midday dinner in the servants' hall by the kitchen, to hear the subway roaring by somewhere behind the basement walls. I imagined tunneling through somehow, putting Rose on a subway train, and sending her to the end of the N line, somewhere in outer Queens.

I studied Mr. Sewell's erratic schedule to the best of my ability, looking for times when he would reliably be out without stopping home to change clothes for the club or take a morning call to Munich. Harder still to predict were those late-night dinners with his mysterious parade of visitors: portly gents who arrived in limousines that parked around the block;

showgirls who poured themselves out of taxicabs; characters who wore their coat collars up and their hats down over their eyes.

Alphonse served at those dinners, but refused to let a word pass on what transpired. In fact, since he'd told me about his life in the Old Country, he had withdrawn, and I got the sense that he regretted saying as much as he had. His eyes followed me as I skulked in the shadows of the house, testing window locks and rattling doors, but whenever I turned to face him, he looked away, refusing to meet my eye.

By the time the worst of Rose's illness had passed, we'd seen Thanksgiving come and go, and I had the skeleton of a plan.

I detailed it in tiny writing on a scrap of paper that I folded and folded and folded again, as if preparing a note to pass under Sister Ignatius's wary eye. It was a simple plan, involving me making a ruckus in front of the house one day, drawing everyone's attention, while Rose smashed a window in her room and escaped over the roof. Although I wasn't sure how she'd get down exactly. Or where she'd go. Or what she'd do next.

By now, I was an expert at distracting Bridie's flittering attention through random observations and compliments that I'd volley her way while she prepared Rose's meal trays. When she turned her back, heaping, I noted, spoonfuls of that benign sugar into Rose's tea, I slipped the bit of paper underneath the slight hollow that formed between Rose's delicate dishware and the silver tray on which it rested.

Up went the dumbwaiter, and because I couldn't risk Bridie finding Rose's response, I stuck by her side, diving back into the dishes. "Well, isn't this a treat to have some company!" Bridie kept exclaiming as I scrubbed at Chef's mounting piles, while he swore under his breath in French at me, afraid I'd corrupt Bridie somehow with my propensity to drop crockery.

"Oh, let me, Bridie dear." I leaped when I heard the familiar squeak of the dumbwaiter, making its return descent. "You take a load off those poor toesies, and let me fix you a cup of tea."

"Well, I never!" she exclaimed, settling down with a sense of luxury on a nearby stepladder. "Really, Martha, a girl could get used to this!"

But any tea was forgotten as I tore apart the lunch tray. The note was gone, but the tray—except for toast crumbs and a few soupy, soggy parsnips—was empty, devoid of any response.

Chapter
18

Bridie found herself a partner in dishes all the way into December, as I kept poring over the returned trays. I sent up other notes—first adapting my scheme slightly, then spitballing new plans one after another—but received nothing in return.

I shortly found out why.

"Dear me, no," Ma answered when I casually asked if Mrs. Sewell ever sent any letters. "Not since she tried to stab Mr. McCagg with a fountain pen last year. No pens or pencils for her, I'm afraid. Dr. Westbrook wanted to prescribe bromides after that. But I told Mr. Sewell no. Not after what I saw happen to Florence Adamo—well. I simply told Mr. Sewell what could happen if she abused those bromides. And he agreed with me—it was too dangerous to start down that road."

So Ma didn't know that Mr. Sewell had secured for his wife a whole cookie jar of "special sugar," dosed out several generous spoonfuls at a time, and turned his maids into dispensaries.

"Calm and quiet, that's all she needs. And look at her now. Quiet as a mouse, she just sits nicely and studies her pictures all day. It's the nicest Christmas present we could have gotten."

So Rose was thinking, too, quietly plotting alongside—or rather above—me.

I kept sending notes. And I waited for Rose to send me an answer, in the form of those pictures she studied so nicely.

I waited through Christmas, with its holly and bright paper in the shops and glittered cardboard angels that fluttered on our drafty windows.

Despite promises in his last postcard, Daddo didn't show, although he did send his friend Stan Pettite (a little person whose Mini-Hercules act "astounds with feats of strength!") to deliver oranges for me and the twins and a ham, which Stan promptly invited himself to help us eat.

Ma and I gave the boys baseball gloves. They gave us some chewing gum they'd bought at the drugstore at the last minute. I gave Ma some cologne I'd bought at Dr. Murphy's shop. She gave me a sensible black tam that looked just right with a maid's uniform. I knew she'd stayed up nights knitting it.

"It's very becoming on you," she nodded, catching a stray strand of hair and returning it to its rightful place. "Very grown-up. I'm only sorry it will cover the lovely hair comb Mr. Sewell gave you."

Mr. Sewell—or rather, Ma—had chosen hair combs for all the female servants in the house. Styled in the shape of butterflies, their wings shone with cloisonné enamel in autumn colors: red, orange, russet. The men had gotten tie pins.

"That's real gold, that is," she said, giving me a kiss on the head where the comb belonged, then turning to climb into her bed. "Mr. Sewell doesn't skimp when it comes to those he values."

I knew Mr. Sewell's definition of "value" differed greatly from mine. What exactly were we being rewarded for? What did he hope we'd "yield"?

As Ma reached for *Jane Eyre*, I knew she'd dream of poor Mr. Sewell and his lonely Christmas. I would dream of Rose.

I waited and plotted through New Year's, pushing past the throngs on the subway bound for Times Square. In this bright new year of 1929, the whole city seemed a party fueled by an extra dash of optimism (and a little bathtub gin). And why not? The stock market bounced as frenetically as the Charleston, but like the hemlines, kept going up. Movies now had sound, thanks to *Steamboat Willie*, and it was only a matter of time before we knew what Charlie Chaplin sounded like. And Mr. Hoover, waiting for his March inauguration, kept promising chickens in everyone's pots.

I eyed the merrymakers wistfully as they headed to their festivities. But as it turned out, the new year had its own party in store for me. And the opportunity I'd been looking for, in the form of a bankrupt British socialite-poetess by the name of Lady Florenzia Smith-Smythe.

Influenza was battering New York that winter, and Ma ruled both home and work by her seesawing health codes: Wash your hands! Keep your hands dry! Air out this room! Don't catch a chill! Get some fresh air in your lungs! Close the door before you catch your death! Ma ordered Chef to juice all the oranges from the trees in the courtyard.

Despite the precautions, members of the Sewell household started falling like tin soldiers, starting with Mr. Sewell. He demanded a bed made up in his office, where he sat for a week, shouting down the telephone and commanding an army of reporters who made pilgrimage to his bedside, all the while roaring, "I am *not* sick! Our health is our greatest wealth! A sound body is the child of a sound mind!"

Next went Ma, her position on the front lines finally catching up with her. By sheer willpower, she crept through each day, shuffling between the Sewells, meeting each of their needs between frequent rests on the stairs. "I just need a cup of tea," she kept insisting breathlessly, her face ghostly gray. I offered to take over her duties with Rose, reaching for her keys. But Ma said she could handle it, if I could take over the menu planning with Chef?

But Chef was toppled, too, and then Bridie, leaving me to fix not only Rose's meals but those for the demanding Mr. Sewell. Luckily chicken soup was all that anyone wanted—servant meals included—so I boiled up all the chickens in the icebox, and when we ran out of those, I simply called down to Katz's

Delicatessen and had them deliver it by the gallon.

By the time Chef could stand upright again, Alphonse was down. But by now, Mr. Sewell was up and puttering, and I got a taste of what his fleet of reporters must put up with every day. Demands for items—newspapers from Hindoostan, fresh handkerchiefs, the address of the attorney general, some health elixir only sold in San Francisco—were lobbed constantly, and admittedly I hid as much as possible, hoping the demands would fly over me and stick to some other barely standing soul.

By five o'clock, I was dead on my feet, but Ma was deader.

"Ma, if you don't get some rest, you're going to end up in your eternal rest. I'm not kidding, Ma. Let me put you in a cab."

She closed her eyes as if she might kip out standing right there, talking to me.

"I know," she squeaked. "I'll—"

A phone rang in Mr. Sewell's office. A few moments later, the master came out, his robe flapping over a collarless shirt and his nose still red. Assistants and subordinates streamed like ants from behind him.

"Mrs. O'Doyle, good, there you are! I'm expecting a guest for dinner. Something elegant, to impress. Let's say three—no, four courses. At eight o'clock. Good!" He clapped his hands and spun back around, slamming the office door behind him.

Ma took a deep, rattling breath. "All right, now, there's Chef to prepare—"

"Ma, no!" I grabbed her by the shoulders. "This is barmy. I'll tell Chef. Go home!"

"But Alphonse isn't—"

"I'll serve at the table. I can do it! I've got a clean apron! And it's forks on the left, fish knives on the outside, and all that." Or was it fish knives on the inside?

Ma nodded weakly and hobbled toward the back stairs. I wasn't sure if she'd agreed or was just nodding off. Either way, I stuck my head out the door and asked Jake, the cop out front, to hail her a taxi. Or to come get me if she didn't appear in the next few minutes.

I rubbed my hands together like a picture show villain. I finally had a front row seat at New York's most exclusive—and mysterious—dinner venue.

Maybe it was post-flu psychosis, or maybe it was the hot brandies he whipped up for himself at the stove. But Chef was all smiles as he embarked on a meal for a king and barely seemed to register that the mustached man usually brandishing the silver trays was now a flushed redheaded girl.

Mr. Sewell seemed in good spirits, too, as he rushed forward to greet the fashionably late Miss Smith-Smythe. Now smartly dressed and shaved, but still with a nose like a stop sign, he pushed past me to be the one to take her coat, a full-length mink, complete with mink feet ready to scurry away as they brushed against the floor.

It was like the lights going up on a picture show, and Miss Smith-Smythe was its star. Everything about her sparkled: her bobbed hair was platinum, her dress an electric peacock blue, her fingers a collection of light-scattering jewels.

"Darling!" she sang out, planting a kiss on each cheek, and then repeating the action. "It's just as I expected, darling. A fairy tale! Show me everything!"

"Something to drink?" said Mr. Sewell, tossing the coat practically over my head like a coatrack. "Martha, get Miss Smith-Smythe—

"Darling! Miss Smith-Smythe is my second cousin who works at a typewriter. Please—it's *Lady* Florenzia."

Mr. Sewell blushed. Blushed! "Ah, Martha, please get *Lady* Florenzia a drink."

I didn't know what Mr. Sewell wanted me to offer, as the house was as dry as a dinosaur bone.

But Lady Florenzia sized this up instinctively.

"Do you have tomato juice?" She said it *to-mah-to*,

like Ma. But not like Ma. "I'm only drinking tomato juice these days. It's all anyone is drinking in Hollywood at the moment. Did I tell you I just got back?"

She steered him to the front parlor, and I left him to give her the tour.

By the time I caught up, they were in the gallery in front of the Rembrandt. I handed over the tomato juice like the maid handing over the goblet of poison, but the irony seemed to escape Lady F.

"Just *look* at this space!" Tomato juice splashed over onto the floor as she gestured, and I noted the spot for cleaning tomorrow. "And it leads to the dining room? *And* to the ballroom?" She flung open the doors opposite and strolled into the great mirrored room, flicking on lights. You could almost see the dancers swirling.

"It's so deliciously *empty*, my dear. Like King Tut's tomb, but with space for an orchestra. Oh, it's just too *too* perfect!" She wrapped herself around Mr. Sewell's arm, while I pressed myself against a wall like a good servant: at the ready, but hoping they'd forget my existence. "How dare you keep this to yourself all this time! Like a naughty boy, refusing to share his toys." She wagged her bejeweled finger at him.

Mr. Sewell flushed. "It's a nuisance, believe me. My father-in-law's idea: throw a lot of gewgaws and marble around, pay people to polish it all day, and then invite a bunch of suck-ups over to congratulate you on it." Despite his best efforts, he finally pulled out his handkerchief to blow his nose noisily. "What a waste. On what I spend on staff alone, I could put that money in the stock market and double it tomorrow."

I was tempted to walk out then and there and let him get his own tomato juice. But then I wouldn't get to eavesdrop.

Miss Smith-Smythe pulled a dramatic frown. "But then I wouldn't have anywhere for my party." She sulked.

"What party?" Mr. Sewell glared.

"Well, you see," and here the lady sashayed out to the center of the ballroom, all too aware of the way the mirrors bounced her sparkling image around the room, "I've planned the most spectacular Mardi Gras masquerade next month. But now Mildred van der Hyden is saying that *she'll* throw one, too, the same night. And she managed to get the Ritz, and the St. Regis is having construction for the next month. So you see,"—she stuck out her rouged lower lip—"I have a party, but no place to go."

"This isn't a place for parties," he said sternly, then cleared his throat. "I have . . . uh, business concerns here I can't have disrupted."

"Well, we're speaking the same language, darling!" She strolled back over to what the three-card-monte guys on the street called the *mark*. "That's why I'm here, to talk business."

Mr. Sewell tucked his hands in his trouser pockets and chuckled. "Do you propose to rent it out like a Knights of Columbus banquet hall?"

Lady Florenzia laughed her own birdlike laugh. "Rent? What do I look like, a grocer? I'm talking about a trade." She put her arm through his again. "Of something you might value."

My stomach churned. I wasn't sure I wanted to know what she proposed to trade. Yet, despite myself, I leaned in.

Lady Florenzia flicked a glance at me. "But perhaps—"

"No, don't worry about that," Mr. Sewell said hurriedly, "go on."

I guessed *that* was me.

"Certain people at this party," she continued in a hushed voice that forced him to lean in, "might have certain information. Information that, depending on how you sing it, could make the market do a little dance, just for you.

"But!" She laughed that tinkling laugh again. "They're not the sort to get comfortable for the

199

first boy who buys them a drink. They need to be romanced. Shown a good time—no, a *bloody* good time. They need to be hosted in a spectacular way, in a way that shows them that *you*"—she walked her fingers up his arm—"*you* understand that they aren't just any source. They're the plum of all prize plums."

And here their heads bent together, murmuring something so sensitive even a servant girl couldn't be trusted with it.

"Ah, I see." Mr. Sewell nodded, and you could see the gears turning in his head. "And just what qualifies as spectacular, in these sources' books?"

It was just the invitation the lady was waiting for. "Well!" She broke off and began striding around the room, her hands conducting an invisible orchestra of lavish spectacle. "In honor of Carnival, we throw a real-live carnival! Masks and costumes, obviously. Coney Island games in all the rooms, but instead of tat we do real prizes—watches and bracelets and other trinkets. I've got a line with Tiffany. Cotton candy stands and roasted peanuts, along with other, uh, libations." She cocked her head, thinking. "The ceiling in here *might* be high enough for a modified trapeze act. But! An orchestra in here for dancing, that goes without saying. I'd get the band from the Cotton Club, and the dancers, too. And we'd do a scavenger hunt at midnight with a real-live treasure chest at the end."

Mr. Sewell looked simultaneously impressed and horrified. Perhaps he was adding up the bill for this spectacular. But Lady Florenzia kept going.

"And let me handle the guest list. I've got the Fitzgeralds and the Pickfords locked up, and the *New Yorker* crowd is always good for a laugh. Eddie Cantor can usually be persuaded to do a set, if you throw in a little sweetening, and I'm sure I could convince Douglas Fairbanks to fly in from California for the occasion." She came back to give Mr. Sewell's arm a squeeze again. "Trust me, darling. The fodder for your paper's gossip column alone will sell a million papers."

This seemed to turn the tide for the businessman. "And your colleagues, the, uh, crown jewels?"

"At the top of my guest list, my dear. We'll set up a war room, just for you and any special guests."

Mr. Sewell smiled like a lion looking at a lame zebra. "Well, then, it sounds like we have details to hammer out. Shall we retire to the dining room?"

Lady Florenzia took a single sip of her glass of *to-mah-to* juice and set it down with a clang on my tray, as if I were a coffee table.

"Oh, I'm not hungry anyway. Let's go out and

celebrate, darling!" She grabbed his arm and pulled him as she swept out of the room. "Louis Armstrong's playing a private set tonight at a place in the Village. . . ."

My heart raced. A party with movie stars, right here! A masquerade, no less, with costumes. With guests milling and circulating and too occupied with their own partying to notice who came or went.

A perfect opportunity to spring Rose loose.

I had to make a plan. I had to somehow get word to Rose. I had to clean up the tomato juice. I had to tell Chef that his four-course creation would once again end up cold and untouched.

But first I had to fall facedown on the floor.

I had the flu.

Chapter
19

For three feverish days, I lay in bed. Whenever I opened my eyes, I didn't know whether I'd be greeted by the light of day or the black of night, whether it would be Ma wiping down my limbs with a damp rag or Mrs. Annunziata spooning soupy rice into my mouth.

I drifted in and out of dreams. One in particular kept coming back for me, pulling me by the hand. Over and over I was trapped in a labyrinth of rooms, the walls covered with pictures of gods and goddesses who whispered to draw closer and cackled when I pressed my ear to their flawless painted mouths. I'd run for the door, just to discover that each door led only to another room, and each window was covered to the top with dirt, the sound of a subway train rumbling somewhere through the cold, sleeping earth.

When the fever broke, and I found myself in bed, Ma sitting in the corner humming and darning by lamplight, it took me a moment to remember whether I was a girl named Martha or Rose.

Whoever I was, I had to find the exit.

As soon as I could stand, I insisted on going back to work. I could tell Ma was impressed by my newfound work ethic, but of course, it wasn't that. I had to get word to Rose of the new plan.

As it turns out, I didn't have to.

Ma must have told her mistress about the upcoming party, whether in excitement or complaints. And according to the painting Rose sent down shortly thereafter, Rose landed in the same place as me.

The regal Sophonisba and her poison chalice were gone, cleared out along with the toxins in Rose's blood. In its place was a single painting. At only about ten inches high, the tiny canvas made the grand gallery look like it had sprouted a blemish. But unlike a pimple, the only word I could use to describe it was flat. It was as if the image wasn't so much painted as glued together out of red, yellow, and pink scraps of paper, like a child's handmade valentine.

And what was the image, anyway? The label claimed them as *Pierrot and Harlequin*, which I knew were the names of circus performers, but it took looking at it from several angles to identify them, and one still looked more like a duck to me. And no matter how much I looked, I wasn't sure why their noses pointed one way and their eyes another, or where one fellow's arm started and another's ended.

"Picasso," the label said. It figured that the same man who turned a pomegranate into lines and squiggles would see a circus act as a melted box of Crayolas.

But one thing was clear: The two figures were wearing masks.

I leaned in to listen to that pip-squeak of a painting: Let's not call attention to ourselves, it whispered. Be inconspicuous. Be inscrutable. Find the right disguise.

From what I gathered from Ma's grumblings, the party promised to be a boisterous affair. Half of New York had been invited, Lady Florenzia insisted: "The perfect combination of the right half, the 'right now' half, and the just-wrong-enough half." Though the math didn't add up, Lady Florenzia, who now visited daily to assess and reassess each room and yammer ever-changing plans at Ma, had no doubt of the party's success.

"Costumes will be de rigueur, darling," she said as Ma waved away the smoke from her ridiculously dramatic cigarette holder. The more I studied Lady Florenzia, the more she resembled less a duchess and more a character inspired by characters mashed together from the pictures. And I was sure I'd heard her accent slip a couple of times, once when Ma—accidentally?—opened a door on her foot, and Her Ladyship uttered an oath I'd never heard outside a Brooklyn tavern.

"We'll turn away anyone without a costume, it's that simple. After all, the theme is Carnival!—more specifically, Coney Island Carnival—and the dress code is Circus Chic. In my experience, it's the costumes that inspire people to truly forget themselves. Speaking of which, did my, erm, contact get in touch?"

I couldn't help but look over at Ma, who took a long, deep breath over her clipboard. I was in prime eavesdropping position, polishing the mirrored walls as Lady Florenzia stalked the ballroom and shouted directions. Two Latvian sisters worked alongside me, brought in for the coming weeks to help get the house in order, and whether they didn't understand the language or just wanted to keep their positions, they didn't look up once from their work.

But I was all ears.

Ma tapped the clipboard, measuring her words before responding. "Have you spoken to Mr. Sewell about these . . . refreshments? Because Mr. Sewell is a law-abiding man, and this has been a godly house since I've been here."

Lady Florenzia stroked my mother's arm like a child's, in the same gesture I'd seen her use with Mr. Sewell. "Of course, my dear! And that's why we have New York's Finest just outside the door, making sure everything stays within these four walls. Now," giving Ma a little side hug, "don't fret. Mr. Sewell understands the need to entertain his guests with style. And you're welcome to prepare some—what? Let's say punch?—for any teetotalers in attendance. Perhaps on a table, over there." She fluttered her sparkling hands at a dark and distant corner in the hallway.

Ma shook her head, but ever the ideal servant, bit her tongue. Mr. Sewell had told Ma to give Lady Florenzia "free rein," and the lady had seized those reins and was riding roughshod over the neat and honorable house Ma had helped build over the years.

But the wilder the party's plans, the sharper in

focus my own plans became. Costumes. Dancing. Gambling. Copious quantities of dubious liquor. There would be enough distraction at this party to allow a herd of elephants to traipse through unnoticed, let alone an unassuming woman in a disguise exiting a dumbwaiter and walking out the front door.

But what disguise exactly? What costume would allow Rose to exit unrecognized—and how would I get my hands on it? And even if she did get out the door, then what? There was that cop outside—maybe more with the event—and there would probably be journalists from rival papers trying to get the evening's scoop. And in the middle of February, it would be freezing, not a night for a stroll.

"Now, entertainment," Lady Florenzia was saying. "We'll have a stage built *here* for the orchestra, and this bit here will be for dancing. And—this is *too too* much, you must agree—I've got the projectionist from The Roxy setting up in the mezzanine to project real-live moving pictures on the gallery walls! We'll transform the art gallery into a nickelodeon!"

She said this like it was a good thing.

"And we have the carney games—the shoot-'em-up, the windup pitch, oh, and a dunk tank!—in the front parlors. But it feels like we just need something else, don't you agree?"

"A freak show!"

As the idea took me, I leaped off my stepladder and let the vinegar-damp rag drop from my hand. "Just like on the boardwalk. You know, wandering contortionists, sword swallowers." I cleared my throat. "A bearded lady."

"Oh, darling." Lady Florenzia crossed over to me and caught up my hands in hers, as if we were long lost friends. "You'd have Scott Fitzgerald dancing with the fat lady, Dorothy Parker toasting King Hottentot, a duet with Cole Porter and a fire breather."

I couldn't tell if she was shocked or delighted.

She threw her arms around me and peppered my face with kisses. "Oh! It's absolutely brilliant! But where to *find* these specimens. . . ."

"Vaudeville," I said too quickly, and avoided Ma's eyes as she stared daggers at me. "Um, we know some vaudeville folks. Maybe we could convince them to do it."

"Well, I'll leave it to you then, um . . ."

"Martha." I smiled as I wiped the lip rouge off with my sleeve. "Of course, there's just the question of price. . . ."

I knew with Lady Florenzia's—or rather, Mr. Sewell's—bottomless budget, I could convince some of Daddo's vaudeville pals to play the freak for the night. There were The Flying Finns and the Boxing Baroulian Sisters. There was Stan, the aforementioned Mini-Hercules, who could lift up to two times his weight. There was even Frau Brunnhilde, an A-above-high-C opera singer who could serve as a fat lady in a pinch.

Then there was Jenny Donovan, better known as Mr. and Mrs. Ballroom, a half-and-half act where she'd dance looking like a lady on one side and a gentleman on the other. Most importantly, she was a tall, skinny thing like Rose. If she doubled her half beard, she'd make a great bearded lady for the night. Then Rose could borrow her costume midway through the party and walk out unnoticed, saving me from finding (or buying) Rose her own costume.

And a gig that paid this much, and had the added bonus of bringing him back to his beloveds, would lure Daddo back to New York, no matter what tour enticed him. There would be no performances by Creak and Eek that night, though. Daddo would be playing a different part: getaway driver, paid to get Rose wherever she wanted to escape.

But tracking down all of these acts would take some work. I needed the help of Daddo's agent, Harry Brownstein-now-Beecham. I remembered

Daddo saying his office was on Twenty-Eighth Street, and with Lady Florenzia's fervent encouragement (and Ma's reluctant permission), I left the rags and mirrors behind.

I was headed to Tin Pan Alley.

Chapter

20

The wind was wailing mercilessly off the Hudson, and when I turned off down West Twenty-Eighth Street, I almost lost my footing, along with the tam Ma'd knitted. After a few futile grabs, I let it fly and instead pulled my scarf over my head.

The last time I'd been on this street, it had been a summer day, and I was holding Daddo's hand. I'd understood immediately why they called it Tin Pan Alley. With the windows all open, the clanging of piano music bounced out of dozens of buildings with dozens of piano rooms hosting dozens of singers and songwriters, all competing to sell the Next Big Hit.

Today the street seemed muffled. Maybe it was the windows shut up against the wind and cold, but as much as I strained my ears, I could only hear a soft, blanketed melody, accompanied by what sounded like a lone saxophone.

I had trouble finding Daddo's agent's office, too. Not only had he changed his name to Beecham, he'd taken on new partners and repainted the door to read:

BEECHAM, BEAUCHAMP & BROUGHAM:
VOICE TALENT OF DISTINCTION

The name may have changed, I thought as I climbed the stairs past ringing phones and practice rooms, but it certainly still fit. Everyone knew Daddo's voice could fill a house up to the rafters. No wonder Harry loved him (even if he didn't always pay him on time).

Last time I'd visited with Daddo, it was just us and a ventriloquist act in the waiting room, plus an old lady receptionist, asleep at her typewriter. But this time I could barely edge past the door. The room was packed with showbiz hopefuls loosening their ties, making gargling sounds in their throats, and reading from papers they rattled in front of them.

"Blancodent! A whiter smile by a mile!"

"*Blancodent!* A *whiter* smile by a mile!"

"Blancodent! A whiter *smile* by a *mile!*"

They weren't as loud as Daddo, but their voices reminded me of Ma's oldest kid gloves, worn so soft they felt like butter in your hand.

"Yes?" A lady in a snappy suit and a very short bob looked at me quizzically. "Can I help you? The agency doesn't represent kids, honey."

I felt out of place in a way I never had alongside tap dancers and ventriloquists. So I yanked the scarf off my head. "No," I said loudly. Too loudly. "I'm here for my father."

"Oh!" she shouted before I could explain further. "Go right in, honey, he's waiting for you." Her hands flapped me toward the back, and she hollered over my head: "Harry, your daughter's here!"

"Wait, no—" I started to turn back, but at that moment, one of the hopefuls burst out of Mr. Beecham's office, flinging his pages to the floor and spitting on them.

"Find another agent then, Shakespeare!" Mr. Beecham called after him, then shouted, "Next up!"

I peeked my head in.

"Wait a second, who're you?"

"Your daughter!" called in the receptionist, who I was beginning to think was not as sharp as her suit would make you believe.

"My daughter? Whaddaya talking about?" he shouted back over my head. "I'm meeting my daughter uptown—" He started to shut the door in my face.

"Wait!" I pushed the door open again. "I'm not your daughter, Mr. Beecham."

"Yeah, no kidding." The door stayed half open, half closed while he looked me up and down. "So what do you want? I'm busy here. I got six more guys to see before supper."

"I'm Martha O'Doyle, Daddo's—I mean, my pop is O'Doyle's O-mazing Spook Show?"

Mr. Beecham knit his fleshy brow like he was doing long division. Then the wrinkles cleared. "Oh, sure, the skeleton act, right? What about it?"

"Well, I know he's doing an out-of-town run, but I need to track him down. You see, there's a very big booking here in the city next month—"

"And what do you want me to do about it?"

I took a deep breath. Daddo was right; agents wanted to take their five percent and give you a nickel to call in the booking yourself. "I was hoping you could tell me what theater he's booked in this week so I could get a telegram to him. And as long as we're talking, I'd like to discuss a very big opportunity coming up for some of your other acts—"

"Wait, you talking about Billy O'Doyle? He's not on the road. I just saw him an hour ago at The Crown Jewel."

"What, here in New York?" I shook my head, the very motion trying to shake loose my understanding. "No, no, he's down South."

"Trust me, kid, I just saw him down on Twenty-Sixth Street."

"What's he doing here?"

He shrugged and started closing the door. "How should I know? I haven't represented vaudeville in years. It's all radio now. Speaking of which—" Mr. Brownstein-now-Beecham squeezed his melon of a head out the door. "Next!" And slammed the door behind him.

The Crown Jewel. It wasn't a theater Daddo'd ever mentioned. As I made my way down the stairs, I tried to wrap my mind around where to begin? That Daddo was around the corner? That he was playing a hall in the city, something he'd been trying to pull off for years? And the big one—that he was here, and we hadn't heard a word?

Maybe he was just stopping off between trains, I thought between the pounding of my heart and the pumping of my legs as I raced those two blocks down Broadway. Maybe he was taking his act straight to the theater manager, now that—another shock—he didn't have his agent anymore.

My eyes scanned West Twenty-Sixth Street up and down, but there were no signs, no names in lights, only drab tenement and warehouse buildings, their rickety fire escapes the only marquee. I started hunting door to door—maybe the theater fronted Twenty-Seventh, with only the stage door on Twenty-Sixth—until I found what I was looking for. An unassuming wooden door, down a few steps, with a folding metal grate pulled across it, and a small hand-lettered sign next to the bell: THE CROWN JEWEL.

I rang, and almost immediately a large man opened the first door only as wide as his face, leaving the grate as a screen between us. He considered me for exactly two seconds, then muttered, "No kids," and began to shut the door.

"Wait!" I banged on the grate. "Wait! I'm looking for Dad—for Mr. O'Doyle. The skeleton act. It's—it's urgent."

The man stepped back. "We got an O'Doyle here?" What dim light existed behind him revealed a sawdust floor and a room of nondescript wooden tables and chairs. The stale smell of beer wafted through the grate. The scene was as familiar to me as a family picture.

A man stood wiping down a bar that ran along the length of the back wall. He stopped just long enough to gesture at one table with his elbow. "There he is."

A lump of clothing covered the table, a skeleton slumped in sympathy on either side.

Daddo.

Chapter
21

I knew from experience that it was best to get Daddo up on his feet and walking in the cold.

Ma used to say—back before she stopped saying anything—that Daddo spent too much time at the saloons. But Ma never understood theater folk, see? She didn't see the bits and gags that Daddo riffed at the bar with his buddies, or the way the men bought Daddo pints when he sang along with the player piano, or the way they all called his name when he walked in the door. In the bar, he was Daddo to everyone.

But yes, sometimes he lost count, and he needed me to get him going again. So we marched up and down Broadway, him stumbling beside me in just a suit jacket and a banged-up top hat. I had Creak and

Eek each slung over my shoulders by an arm, dragging their bony feet along the sidewalk.

Even for New York, we got some strange looks.

Still, while I'd found Daddo in plenty of speakeasies, I'd never found him in the wrong state, and I tamped down the furious confusion just under my chest, breathing slowly to keep it from flinging words out of my mouth. I let him get in seven blocks of sobering arctic blasts before saying a word.

"Daddo."

He jumped as if he'd forgotten I was there. "Oh, my sweet Marty." He threw an arm around me— which is to say, me and Eek. "How good you are to come and see your pop."

"It's a sheer miracle I found you," I said between gritted teeth. "I thought you were in Alabama, after all."

"Alabama, yes indeed. '*Chattanooga, Tuscaloosa, climb on board this train's caboose-a*,'" he began to sing. "I just got back, my girl. Never seen so many grits in my life."

"Chattanooga's in Tennessee. And I already know Harry fired you."

His mouth opened and closed, grasping for words like a fish gasping for air.

I shook my head, and when I caught my reflection in a shop window, I looked just like Ma.

"Vaudeville isn't what it used to be, my girl, my

pearl, my wee O'Doyle." They all rhymed when he said them. His accent clanged in my ears after those velvety radio voices back in Harry's office.

"The big houses don't want the old acts anymore. They just want a laugh, a bit of song-and-dance to open for the picture shows." He stopped to lean against a brick wall, fishing in his pockets for a cigarette and coming up empty, "Well, you know I don't open. I'm a headliner, I am."

"Be honest now. Were you on tour at all? Or were you just on the drink?"

"Now, don't go begrudging your old man a few drinks, for '*With a gallon of whiskey at his feet, and a bottle of porter at his head . . .*'"

"I'm getting tired of your old songs," I snapped. "I think I'm ready for you to start singing a different tune." A blast of cold air blew my skirts around, and I wriggled away from Daddo to hold them down. "Oh, what is Ma going to say."

"Well, my darlin', wait till you hear this tune." He cleared his throat, then got down on one knee, like Al Jolson. "'*Be it ever so humble, there's no place like home . . .*'"

I yanked his arm and got him moving past the beat cop who was starting to slow his gait as he passed. "All right, all right. What are you saying, Daddo?"

220

"Don't you know why I was in that speak? Why, I was celebrating! Celebrating the new act!"

I looked at him suspiciously. "What new act?"

"The one that's going to bring me back to New York! You're right that Harry and I had a parting of ways, but trust me, it was for the best. He's in bed with radio these days. Doesn't understand the draw of the stage, and never did.

"But now I'm working on a new act. What d'you think I'm doing in these clothes, sure?" He dusted off the top hat, which was going green on the edges where the black silk had worn thin. "Oh, it's gonna be grand! It's me and Stan, see? And we're gonna call it—well, we're still working on the name—but I'm thinking something like The Long and the Short of It."

I chuckled despite myself, because Daddo was tall and lanky and looked like his whole body was hung from a coat hanger, and Stan was short and round and bald and pink like a rubber ball. Put them together, and they'd look like an exclamation point.

"The gist is that we're two bums, but Stan is the brawn and I'm the brains, and we do a whole comedy routine where he holds me up on a chair while I recite the Gettysburg Address."

I had to admit, it sounded pretty good. "Yeah,

and you could get some good slapstick in there, like the Keystone Cops."

"Yes, my girl, that's it!" And as a way of testing it out, he walloped me over the head with his top hat, which just happened to be already broken at the crown. This was the Daddo I loved, the one who'd stop in the middle of the street to work out some footwork, or juggle the groceries, or serenade a newsboy. "So Stan and me are polishing up the act. Now alls we need is a venue. Because if the right people see this, we could be bigger than Amos and Andy. I just know it."

My foot started tapping, and my mind started racing.

"The right people? How about society and business types, all in one place? Writers, money men, even film stars!"

"Sounds all right, my girl. You got the key to Sam Goldwyn's office?"

"No." I smiled as it all came together in my mind. "It's a party, at Ma's employer's house. They need entertainers, circus and vaudeville types. They'll have all kinds of swells there. And it's good money!"

He shook his head while he coughed and spit. "You really think your ma would let me come to her precious place of employment? Like this?" Daddo flapped the sides of his shabby suit jacket.

"Trust me, she's been vetoed on everything from the menu to the dress code. She can't say a thing." I stopped on the sidewalk, making him look in my eye. "But look, if you want the gig, there are a few requirements."

"Sure, sure, Marty. Anything for my new manager!" He swept me up in a waltz, flinging skeletal limbs into the huddled bundles that hastened past us out of the wind.

"This is serious, Daddo." I stopped him again and slung Eek over his shoulder, making him share the load as we pushed forward down Broadway. "First of all, you gotta get some of your friends to come, pretend to be sideshow freaks for the night. Jenny Donovan especially."

"Huh." He rubbed his chin. "Well, I'll tell ya, I haven't seen the old gang in a while."

"It's nonnegotiable," I said, my hands on my hips. "No Jenny, no Daddo and Stan. And Jenny's got to bring a full beard."

Daddo chuckled. "You drive a harder bargain than Harry. All right, all right, I'll chase up some freak acts I know."

"Good. The more circus-y, the better. And I'll have a job for you afterward. Not a gig, just a favor." I made my voice sound nonchalant, as if this weren't the most important piece. "You'll need to borrow a car for the night."

"Well, sure. Cloaky McClure owes me a favor, and he's got a workhorse Model T he's always bragging about, God knows why—"

"And here's the last thing." I stopped and held him at arm's length. "You come home. You stay off the road, and you take a break from the drink. You stay the straight and narrow and make up all these absences to Ma." To us.

He squirmed. Squirmed. My heart froze to see that he regarded this as the last straw.

I pushed the thought out of my mind and determined to push it out of his, too. "Think, Daddo. Home-cooked meals, Ma darning your socks, and the boys jumping on you every morning in bed." He smiled, and I saw his eyes go a bit moist. "We might could even get some money up front, rent a studio, let you and Stan work out your act in peace and quiet."

"Sounds grand," he said quietly, pulling Eek's arms around his neck tighter like a woolly muffler. "It'll be a new beginning."

I put my arm through his, and as we walked toward the R train, I chose to believe him.

Chapter
22

" This is the last thing I have time for!" Ma fretted as Alphonse lugged a large canvas through a swarm of caterers, florists, servants, and servers.

The party hadn't even begun yet, and Ma was at her breaking point. It wasn't just the party preparations, with the endless rounds of menus with Chef, and the counting the silver and tracking down the crystal that had Ma aflutter. We'd had to take on two extra maids just to wake the house from its long slumber, plus six new footmen to serve on the night, and a whole brigade of kitchen help to keep the food flowing. We'd gone from a small and reluctantly functional family to a full-blown military operation, and Ma was struggling to keep the battle plans on track.

And she didn't even have an epic escape to plan. A twinge of panic grabbed at my stomach as I watched the frame make its way toward the gallery. What was Rose up to? Was she making a new plan? I'd already sent up notes with the details of my scheme. I needed Rose to commit to the plan, not change the details by way of some picture of a cupid frolicking with forest nymphs—or whatever it was.

With a glance over my shoulder and assured that Ma was occupied with a dropped tray of oysters Rockefeller, I followed Alphonse to the gallery.

I found him in front of the painting, rocking back on his heels and narrowly missing a tray of crystal champagne flutes and a trombone player looking for the bathroom.

"Funny, no?" He chuckled to himself. "Mrs. Sewell still has her humor."

The painting looked like any other to me: another god, wrapped in a bedsheet, leaves in the hair, surrounded by fruit, offering a goblet of wine.

"Bacchus."

"Aha," I nodded, still not seeing what was so funny about it. "God of—"

Alphonse smiled at my attempt. "Wine." In the ballroom, the jazz orchestra began tuning up with barn-like bleating. "And wild revels."

He stroked his mustache, as if trying to fluff it up, though it had filled out nicely. In fact, in his full livery, he looked rather dashing, and you'd never guess just a few years before he'd been on a boat from the Old Country.

Ma had drawn the line at costumes for the servants, especially when Lady Florenzia suggested a skintight acrobat getup. I scratched at my own taffeta "formal," the stiff starched white collar already rubbing my neck raw.

"Ah. Well, isn't that clever," I said flatly. Oh, Rose, I thought, is this really the best time for jokes about mythology? Couldn't we stay focused?

The plan was simple. Daddo, Stan, and Jenny Donovan had worked up an act and were scheduled to go on around eleven thirty. After their spot, they'd change out of their costumes, and Daddo would go pull the car around. I'd go up in the dumbwaiter to Rose's room, where she'd change into Jenny's bearded lady costume. Down we'd go again, one at a time in the dumbwaiter, to the first floor, where I'd escort her out to the sidewalk, into Daddo's borrowed car, and on to—

Where? I didn't know. Daddo had instructions to drive as far as the night and a tank of gas could take them. On the backseat was an old suitcase with some of Ma's castoffs and five dollars I'd skimmed from the Ovaltine can.

The rest was up to Rose.

A servant at the end of the gallery clinked and clanked bottles as he set up one of the six bars I'd counted so far. "I don't think we really need a reminder of what's on the drinks menu."

"It is not the wine. And it is not for us." Alphonse glanced around. "It is for them—the party guests. So they can see who he really is."

"Him?" I pointed at Bacchus.

"Mr. Sewell, of course."

"But Mr. Sewell doesn't drink."

"He does not need to. Notice—he's offering *us* the wine. And tonight, they will all be drinking it."

And with a wave of his hands, the front bell rang, as if Alphonse had summoned the first guest himself.

Not that anyone took two beans of notice of our friend Bacchus, god of wine or no. Why would anyone look at art when there were trapeze artists whizzing from the gallery ceiling?

Or carnival games, with a chance to win real gold watches, diamond earrings, a boat cruise to Bermuda leaving at midnight?

Or a full jazz orchestra from Harlem, playing

music designed to make every society matron think she was Josephine Baker?

Or the year's biggest film star in a dunk tank? Or a senator and a gangster in a Siamese twin costume, or a World Series slugger doing the Black Bottom with the Four-Legged Woman?

I could barely collect the coats fast enough, great piles of furs—like being smothered by zoo animals—that I ferried from guest to cloakroom, hustling to get back to The *Greatest* Greatest Show on Earth.

And then there was liquor: prime stuff, and a hundred percent illegal. The party was drenched in it. Trays of glasses—highballs, low balls, flutes, coupes, tulips—filled and emptied as if on command, and the parquet floors got sloshier as the night went on.

Mr. Sewell hovered above it all, looking deeply uncomfortable in the glossy ringmaster costume Lady Florenzia had selected, as if he couldn't wait to kick out everyone and lock down his fortress again.

"Infernal, egregious waste of resources," he muttered, clenching a glass in hand—no Bacchus here, as his decidedly unmerry demeanor suggested seltzer water. He tapped his foot, waiting for something to happen in a room where everything was happening. "By God, this had better pay off."

Luckily Lady Florenzia had just arrived, fashionably late to her own party, of course. After trading her fur wrap for a boa—a real boa constrictor to complete her snake charmer costume, all shimmer and shimmies—she twined her snaked-wrapped arms around his. I stuck close, pretending to rearrange the furs in my arms.

"I was just saying that this had better pay off," he launched in, dodging her kisses on each cheek. "Just look at these drunken freeloaders—"

"Why, darling, these are your guests! Or if it helps," she said with a wink, "just think of them as potential sources."

"Yes, I know, but . . ." He grimaced as what appeared to be a giant and a midget hobo wandered by. "My God, what a ragged lot."

It was Daddo and Stan, dressed for their act.

"Marty, it's a disaster," Daddo launched in with no notice of the house's ringmaster. "They're squeezing us between Eddie Cantor and Al Jolson!"

Stan readjusted his cap and folded his arms. "We're headliners, we are!"

Lady Florenzia couldn't help but overhear this, and her gaze shifted to Daddo and Stan with disdain. "Is this one of the acts you brought in?" she asked me accusingly.

"Lady,"—Daddo was determined to take his case

to the top—"we're used to the top billing. What're Cantor and Jolson gonna do, just sing? Me and Stan do it all—sing, dance, comedy, you name it. I mean, just look at this."

And there followed a display of the most frenzied and grotesque slapstick.

Just when I thought it couldn't get worse, Jenny Donovan, our Bearded Lady, wandered by. She'd extended her fake half beard to wrap across her face, but with an unmatched hair color, which apparently she hoped to distract from with a most shockingly low-cut gown.

"Fellas, fellas,"—she was already slurring—"getta loada this hooch. 'S'all free, canyastandit?" She swiped another glass from a passing tray.

Mr. Sewell made a sound of contempt from the depths of his throat. "My word, this is—"

I shot Lady F. a look that said, "Let me handle this," and dragged the trio to a corner.

"Look, I didn't want to say anything. Al Jolson—he, uh, he requested you. He heard about your act, and he said, look, I need a little comedy to warm up the crowd, see?" I leaned in conspiratorially. "Maybe if you really kill it tonight, he'll take you on the road? I hear he's headed to Hollywood to make a new talkie. . . ." I let that one dangle.

Stan elbowed my dad in the knees. "The kid's got a point. C'mon, we've got a captive audience. Let's give 'em a preview." And Stan pushed Daddo into the center of the room, where he proceeded to climb him like a telephone pole and beat him about the head with his cap. Jenny pretended to swing punches at Daddo while he held her at arms' length. Daddo shouted his new catch phrase, "Everything's swell, kids!"

No one noticed.

My relief lasted only an instant.

"Miss Smith-Smythe," Mr. Sewell was saying, "you promised me certain meetings. And I promised you use of my house for this travesty, ensuing delivery of said meetings. But if you don't hold up your end of the bargain, I have no qualms about clearing this house. The Fire Department can always be called for signs of a gas leak. . . ."

"Please, call me Lady Florenzia." Miss Smith-Smythe smiled through clenched teeth. "And— Oh!" She exclaimed as a squared-off hunk of granite entered and was relieved of his overcoat. "Speak of the devil, and the devil appears. As it were. Allow me to make the introductions."

And as the serpent slid its way around Lady Florenzia's shoulders, she wound one arm through Mr.

Sewell's and the other through the mystery man's. She moved the real party to the office, where the door was firmly shut to protect whatever sacred knowledge they shared.

I turned and saw Ma, staring suspiciously after the group. She'd had a look all night as if she smelled something rancid, but now she looked—shaken. It was something about the way Lady Florenzia's arm had snaked through Mr. Sewell's.

Between the frenzied pace of clearing coats and plates and the free entertainment, the next few hours flew by.

As their sobriety fell away, so did the guests' disguises, and soon the true behavior of New York's rich and powerful was on full display. Any delusions I had of the rich being more genteel or refined than us common folk were discarded that night, along with the contents of Cole Porter's stomach and the toupee I saw Mrs. Astor fling out a window.

But with pride I saw that the drunker the guests became, the more the servants' smooth sailing stood in relief. Ma had choreographed a beautiful dance, putting the staff through their paces in the weeks preceding so that they parried and glided around the stumbling obstacles, balancing tinkling trays as if by levitation, magically producing fresh drinks and empty ashtrays.

Sometime before midnight my own routine was interrupted by a tug at my elbow. It was Stan, now in a very dapper tuxedo. He shoved what looked like a silk-wrapped badger pelt into my hand. Jenny's beard and costume.

"We bombed," he offered, before I could ask. "We still get paid though, right?"

My eyes scanned the room frantically. Jenny was beardless but tuxedoed, asleep and drooling in a wing chair. "Where's Daddo?"

"'Ere I am, my girl," came a Brooklyn braying behind me, and when I turned I saw Daddo, his costume crumpled beyond what was necessary. "Just celebrating a job well done. Had 'em eating out of our hands, din't we, Stanny Boy?" The glass in his hand jingled merrily with ice cubes and an elixir of dubious origins.

"You find the bar then?" Stan made his dinner jacket dance with a hand on each lapel. "I'm headed that way meself."

"No, no, no," I sputtered, grabbing the drink out of Daddo's hand and pouring it into a potted palm. "You're supposed to be bringing the—"

"Car around, 'course." Daddo's eyes were ringed red, whether from drink or tears I didn't know.

I grabbed Daddo's arm. "Swear, Daddo. Swear you'll do this, and do it right."

Daddo threw a sweaty arm around me. "Now, now, darlin'. When my girl asks, I answer." He gave me a final squeeze. "Just leaving to get it now." Daddo made a retreat through the crowd, but I saw him swipe a champagne glass off a gliding waiter's tray.

I pulled Stan back by his jacket. "*One* drink, Stan. *One*. You have to see to it—"

"See to what? Oh, hello, Stan. Fine show tonight." Ma stepped in, and Stan made a hasty exit. Ma's usually placid forehead glowed with sweat, and she dabbed it with the handkerchief she kept up her sleeve. "Where have you been? I've been looking for you. The sword swallower and Mr. Chaplin made a wager, and now there's blood all over the music room carpet."

"Ma, Daddo's act was—"

"A disaster, I know." She shook her head. "The act was all right, but to follow Eddie Cantor, *ach*—" Ma's eyes looked so sad that the room seemed to deflate for a moment. "These last few weeks at home. I did hope—well, never mind." Ma looked quizzically at the beard in my hands. "What's that?"

"So there's blood in the music room?" I sidestepped.

"Yes, you'll need seltzer." She spotted some breach of etiquette across the room and turned to squelch it. "But first stop by the butler's pantry. I need you to carry the soiled glasses down to the kitchen. The dumbwaiter can't keep up."

The dumbwaiter.

I raced to the pantry and finally saw what I hadn't wanted to see. Waves of platters and trays crashed in and out of the dumbwaiter, filled, then emptied. The rising and falling box was in constant use, manned on either end by servants circulating replenishments and sure to notice even the smallest hitch in its operation, not to mention a Bearded Lady sitting on the canapes.

How could I have overlooked it? How could I have been so stupid? With no dumbwaiter, there would be no way to get Rose's costume to her, and Rose herself would be left waiting, waiting, waiting all night, just as she had for years, as the opportunity for her escape slipped away. The weeks of planning drained out of me, puddled around my feet like a snowman in the sun.

In the absence of a plan, I, for once, did what was asked of me and grabbed trays of dirty glassware to bring down to the kitchen. Not even Bridie gave me a hello in that underground ant farm of activity, where it was hard to say what rattled the dishes more: the jazz music or the rushing of the subway train just outside. I rushed to escape back above deck.

But on my way back to the stairs, I passed Ma's sitting room and was shocked to hear a man's voice inside.

I pushed the door open.

"You got someone to take this down? Okay, here goes: *Film stars, debutantes, and former presidents*—we might have trouble with Taft's people on that one—*former presidents gathered for a night of staggering*—heh, staggering, that's good—*staggering excess at J. Archer Sewell's residence last night.* Full stop. *In a circus-themed blowout that would have shocked Marie Antoinette, New York's glitteratti tried their hand at trapeze and the latest Jazz dance crazes, fueled by libations lately frowned upon by Congress*—"

A short guy in a shabby attempt at a nice suit was on Ma's telephone, usually reserved for calls to the grocer. A mask had been pushed up on his forehead, replaced by spectacles jammed on a stubbed snub nose, and although he looked familiar, I couldn't quite place him. He peered intently at a stenographer's notepad in the lamplight.

The notepad I recognized as a promotion piece the newsstand had given away at Christmas: NEWS TO YOU? read the cardboard cover. READ THE *YODEL*!

Lady Florenzia had been very clear: no press. But more importantly, no one was allowed in Ma's sitting room except Ma.

"Hey! You can't be in here."

"S'all right, kid. Go back upstairs." He turned his back to me and pressed his lips back to the receiver. "Okay, picking up with *In her younger days*—"

"Hey! You're not supposed to be here. Not *here*," I jutted my chin toward the room, "or here at all, mister. No press."

"Look, I gotta get this in before the three a.m. press run. So just run along—"

"I'll run along, and I'll get one of the guys out front." Mr. Sewell had stationed some guys with ham necks by the door to check invitations and keep out fellows just like this.

The man shoved his notepad into his breast pocket. "Look," he fumed into the receiver, "I gotta find another phone. Don't print anything without my say-so." He slammed down the phone and pushed past me, not noticing when his notepad got knocked to the floor. I kicked it spitefully into a corner and followed him up the back stairs, intending to see him out the trade entrance, but got caught behind two footmen balancing silver bowls of ice cream for the dessert service.

"Some shindig, huh," said the slick-haired Irishman in front of me.

"I'll say," came back a voice by way of Bensonhurst. "Just saw Babe Ruth passed out under the pianah, all tree-hunderd pounds of 'im." Bensonhurst stopped to swipe a trail of melting ice cream with his finger. "Put yer money on the Dodgers this year, boys!"

And just like that, I had a new plan.

"No, no, no, no," Ma chanted as we made our way to the ballroom. Sure enough, Babe Ruth lay snoring under the grand piano like a beached whale. A beached whale at a raucous jazz spree where no one gave any notice to whales, beached or otherwise.

"How are we—"

"McCagg!" I burst in before she could finish the thought. "He's the only one big and strong enough."

She thought for a minute, assailed from all sides by foxtrotting couples. "All right. Go get him. I'll get Alphonse to help, too." She turned to leave.

One down.

"Oh, and Ma! Almost forgot. I found some reporter type in your sitting room. Didn't you lock it up?"

Ma looked momentarily furious with herself. "Lord, I must've forgotten."

"Quick, gimme your keys. I'll run down and lock it."

Ma's hands flew to her keys protectively.

"I'll bring them right back. Come on, Ma." I looked back over at the beached Babe as a trombone blast blew my hair askew. "We can't leave him here. Especially with a reporter sneaking around and using your phone."

I had the keys. I had both Ma and McCagg occupied, I had Mr. Sewell behind closed doors, and a house full of partygoers oblivious to anything but their own good time.

Now I just needed Rose.

The key turned easily in the lock on Rose's room. Like everything else in the house, Ma kept it in good working order.

Her room was dark—pitch-black, really—and as I closed the door behind me, I wondered how she could sleep with the thumping and blasting of the orchestra, which vibrated through the house.

"Rose?" I whispered.

A hand—cool, thin—grasped mine.

"I'm ready."

Rose didn't speak as she dressed. Far from the crazed, brutish animal I first saw kicking at the bed curtains, or the catatonic rag doll that couldn't leave her chair, this version of Rose was composed, fixed on the events at hand. She took the Bearded Lady costume from me quickly, whisking off her nightgown and yanking the dress into place.

As she dressed she asked simple questions, pushing ahead when I rambled my answers. Was Mr. Sewell occupied? Was there a car waiting? How long would she have it? She handed me a hatbox. Inside was stuffed a silk dress and some stockings and undergarments, all too fine and out of season, but the only things left in her armoire, I imagined. I resolved to steal her a fur coat.

"Are you sure you have everything?" I asked, clutching the bag.

She pulled the ridiculous beard up and didn't even turn her head. "I've always had everything. Now I have what I need."

Chapter
23

It always seemed fitting to me that the next day was Ash Wednesday.

I knelt bone-tired at the altar that morning. Father Riordan smudged a cross on my forehead, "Ashes to ashes, dust to dust." Ma stared straight ahead, her face unreadable.

I relished my gnawing hunger, happy to use the day's fast as a constant reminder of my sins. I welcomed the ashy sign of my wickedness. I stared straight back when non-Catholics looked quizzically at me on the subway, weighing whether to tell me I had something on my forehead, as if it were spinach in my teeth. Yes, I am a sinner, I wanted to tell them. I wanted to be like God. I wanted to know everything, and I wanted to control it. But I am flawed, and apparently so is everything I touch.

My stare drove their eyes away, and they flicked back to their newspapers, the *Yodel* headlines gloating:

MIDNIGHT RUN!

Wild Rose Stops Traffic!

Did Sewell's Jazz-Crazed Carnival Finally Drive Wife Out of Her Gourd— and Out of Her House?

By the time Rose and I crept down the stairs last night, the party was at a frenzied pitch. Duke Ellington had shown up and commandeered the orchestra to the carnival-goers' delight. Wild rhythms had driven dancers to the tops of antique tables and divans (until yesterday draped to protect their delicate surfaces from the threat of sunlight), or into the arms of real or costumed carnies, while other luminaries leaned uneasily against doorways, plotting how to cross from Point A to B without tipping over.

Just as I predicted, Rose—bearded—would go completely unnoticed.

I pushed Rose forward into the ballroom crowd, then pulled her back almost immediately. Trying to cross that churning sea of dancers doing the Charleston was simply too dangerous; I didn't want Rose's beard getting knocked off midway.

I grabbed Rose's arm, pulling her behind me down the main hall as I threaded around the land mine of partygoers. Did they know her behind that beard, I wondered, as we bumped past New York's brightest lights? Did they miss her presence, these "old friends" of Rose, who once attended her father's salons and social teas, or wonder if she missed them, up in her lonely rooms? If they did, they gave no indication, looking only to the bottom of their bottomless highball glasses.

My eyes were locked on the front vestibule at the end of the hall, and I felt Rose's step falter behind me just as I stopped short of our destination. Sewell stood square in front of us, shaking the block of granite's hand heartily to seal some deal. Lady Florenzia hung her arms on each man's back as if to take credit for the treaty, while her boa flicked its tongue at Mr. Sewell's collar.

Rose and I stood frozen for a moment, reassessing our plan. We had only to lie low, I thought, stay outside their gaze. There was no reason to panic, I repeated to myself unconvincingly. If we just waited for Mr. Sewell to take his leave of his guest, he'd brush past the bearded Rose like any other "nobody" and retire to quiet victory in his office.

Rose's pulse raced under my fingertips, but I also felt her arm rise and fall slightly as she took long, deep breaths to calm herself. I joined her, and we stood there in the rising and falling, the quiet eye of a swirling hurricane, waiting for the scene with Sewell to resolve.

Finally the granite man took his leave. But Sewell didn't retreat to his fortress as expected. Instead he gleefully clapped and rubbed his hands, swiped a drink of God-knows-what off a tray, and downed it in one swallow. Then he tipped Lady Florenzia back, snake and all, and planted a kiss on her like Rudolf Valentino.

Two gasps sounded out like a shot in that moment, the same moment when the orchestra took a long pause meant to set up a dramatic drum solo.

Just behind my left shoulder stood my mother, her mouth still gaping. The look of shock on her face was already beginning a slide through heartbreak, betrayal, and fury.

The other, in retrospect, was more of a guffaw than a gasp, a loud "Ha!" that bubbled out of Rose's throat, and she immediately clapped a hand over her mouth, as if she could will it back inside.

Too late. That scornful laugh must have been her signature, back in the days when she was unafraid to show her disdain for princesses and politicians equally. Back when she believed she had all the power in the world.

I dropped Rose's wrist.

I took one step back.

Mr. Sewell stood up slowly, releasing the shocked snake charmer and turning his head to our little group. He looked hard at the now-shaking Bearded Lady. He walked over, his eyes meeting Rose's over her mustache.

The drum solo was now in full swing, but we all seemed frozen in silence, until the front door opened again, Alphonse and McCagg stamping the snow off their shoes. Their arms hung weary at their shoulders; it must have taken all their strength to get Babe Ruth into a cab.

Maybe that's why their reflexes were slow when Rose made a run for the open door.

She flew past them to the sidewalk, with McCagg, Alphonse, Sewell, Ma, me, even Lady Florenzia behind her.

She dodged and sprang around the surprised

cops who expected to keep reporters out, not heiresses in. Her legs were like a newly born colt finding its footing, trotting and wobbling up and down the curb, banging her hands on every car parked up Fifth Avenue.

I looked, too, scanning the line of limousines waiting for their precious cargo, seeking Rose's target: a barely functional Model T with Daddo at the wheel.

There was none to be found. Daddo wasn't there.

By now the men had her surrounded: the cops with their nightsticks, grabbing at her limbs; Alphonse looking uncertain; McCagg looking determined; not to mention the reporters with their notepads and photog pals with their blinding, flashing cameras.

One reporter—the one I'd kicked out of Ma's sitting room—stood a bit aloof from the pack. His spectacles had been discarded now, and he wore a fedora, shading his eyes from the light of the flashbulbs.

A second wave of recognition washed over me as I remembered that nose poking out under that hat last fall, at the servants' entrance. A source, Ma had called him, as he had pushed inside for an off-the-record meeting with Mr. Sewell.

I saw his eyes under his hat brim now as they

looked at something—someone—behind me: Mr. Sewell, who stood safely out of the fray in the door frame. He gave a slight nod to the reporter, and when I turned back, the reporter was walking away quickly, jotting in a notebook—he must have had an extra—all the way down the street.

A *Yodel* reporter in Mr. Sewell's pocket? But before I could even register the shock, I was pushed aside by McCagg and some of the cops, each holding Rose by a limb and dragging her back inside.

Ma flew to the front door, squeezing between McCagg and Mr. Sewell.

"Take her straight to the back stairs," she hissed. "Get her up the back quietly."

But Mr. Sewell blocked their progress and offered something else in a low voice to McCagg.

The group changed direction then and pushed their way through the partygoers, winding their way through the most public rooms, dragging Rose between them like a lamb tied to a spit.

"I'm being held!" Rose shouted, attempting to be heard over the party's din. "He's holding me prisoner! He won't let me out!"

But rather than inciting an army to her defense, Rose left in her wake only bemused or repulsed party guests, some whispering, some giggling, some shaking their heads, some looking up then deliberately looking away. The mayor seemed asleep on his feet, but roused when the group pushed by. "Whas she say?" he slurred, then slumped down again in a heap against the door frame. A woman dressed as an acrobat—in a flesh-colored body stocking that made her look naked but covered in crystals—dissolved into tears against a—man?—wearing a gorilla costume. "We were best friends once," she wailed into his furry chest. "Best, best of friends! Now look at her!"

And at least half the guests were too caught up in the swirling circus to even notice.

I turned back to Ma, now on the front steps, her jaw clenched in silent rage, her arms crossed as if they alone kept all the fury inside her at bay.

"Ma," I whispered. "Ma, I tried—"

"That man," she muttered between those locked teeth. "How could I have—How did I—" She left whatever she was feeling unfinished, unsettled, and I wasn't sure if she was talking about the reporter, or Mr. Sewell, or Daddo, or maybe all of them.

Not a word passed between Ma and me for the rest of the night. But when we finally got home, in the dark before dawn, when the celebrations of Mardi

Gras were turning to ashes, we didn't need any words. Without even getting undressed, we carried the twins to Ma's big bed and all climbed in together.

I knew now that this was our family. That Daddo wasn't really a father, let alone an actor, but a drunk. A drunk hiding behind a story of bookings and tours, aided by Ma, who figured it was better for kids to have a pretend father than a real void.

So I closed my eyes, with the twins on one side and Ma on the other, and waited for the sun to return.

Chapter
24

By the time March rolled around, everything was looking up.

At least, that's what the papers said, and they were never wrong, were they?

Hoover was finally inaugurated president, promising prosperity for one and all. An astrologer in the papers said the same and assured her clients, including Charlie Chaplin and even J. P. Morgan, that the market would keep going up up up. The *Daily Standard* featured a different company every day, each one promising to make the Next New Thing (and to the savvy, promise the Next Big Stock Tip). The *Yodel* splashed advertisements of shiny new cars and appliances and invited you to buy on credit, no matter what your lot in life.

"Now anyone can live like a millionaire!" the advertisements crowed.

The more time I spent in that hollow and haunted house, the more I thought: Who would want to?

After the party, we started shedding staff like cargo rolling off a sinking ship. Chef suffered a collapse, whether from overwork or overdrink I never knew. As soon as the last of the party's canapés had been plated, he staggered out in the wee hours of the morning and never came back. The silent Magdalena left a letter in her place one morning, claiming a brother offering a job out West. (Her English was near perfect, it turns out.) Bridie spoke officially of an ailing mam back home, but whispered to me as she wrapped the strings around her apron, "It's cursed, this house. There's some black pishogue 'round here, and I wouldn't stay for love or money."

Ma replaced no one. With no more parties, no visitors, and most days no Mr. Sewell, Ma and I soldiered on. Any evidence of that tragic traveling carnival disappeared. The house was put back to sleep, the furniture under billowing white shrouds. The courtyard, which just weeks before had been coaxed into such brilliance for the party, with wild, brash blossoms and ripe fruit, slumped and shed its bounty to be swept into the bin.

Perhaps the flowers just did what flowers do: burst into life, then fade into a finish, dropping exhausted to the floor. Or maybe Ma simply forgot to call the gardeners. Ma's full attention, once again, was on Rose. Ma went quiet at that time, speaking only to direct me to one task or another. She climbed the stairs each day, carrying the shots Dr. Westbrook had recently prescribed to keep Rose calm and a copy of the *Daily Standard* under her arm to pass the hours by Rose's bedside. "But," I sputtered when I first saw the syringe, "didn't you say that bromides—"

"These aren't bromides," Ma cut me off. "And this is none of your concern. You wouldn't understand, so please leave this to the adults." And with that, I understood the source of the eerie stillness that had returned to the top floor and had settled back down into the house's bones.

Still, under the quiet, something was churning.

Alphonse was disturbingly quiet, too. He avoided my eyes when we passed in the hall and left the room when I entered. In his eyes, I saw the guilt of the innocent bystander. Because we both knew: if he'd only helped me—if he'd abandoned his belief that nothing made any difference so why bother, just for one evening—Rose would be free now.

In need of something to hold on to, we all returned to our routines. Mr. Sewell was either at his stockbroker's or at the newspaper office, even sleeping there some nights, if his still-made bed in the morning meant anything. He returned home only to consult with Dr. Westbrook. There were more visits from the doctor, more whispering between the men. "She's a danger, and always has been, and now everyone knows it," Mr. Sewell insisted one morning as I helped the doctor off with his coat. "It's time she was in a place where no one else can be hurt by her actions." The ground under the hallowed doctor seemed to be shifting, and through the office door, I overheard him wearily uttering words like "court-ordered" and "incompetent," plus "sanitorium" and other ominous Latin terms.

For days I waited with clenched stomach for Sewell to demand answers: How did Rose get out that night of the party? But days, then weeks went by with Mr. Sewell passing me in the hall. No words were ever exchanged.

In the end, I realized he didn't care. The outcome was better than any he could have planned, with Rose's madness dragged on display for all of New

York society. Who would doubt him now that his wife was really and truly mad?

And who would guess that her madness was of his own design? To all of New York society, he was the model of the self-sacrificing husband, so in love with his wife he couldn't bear to let her be removed from her childhood home—until it became entirely unavoidable, of course.

It was a story you'd never read in the *Standard*. Of course you wouldn't; why would the paper's owner allow scandalous reports about his own wife? But any *Yodel* reader would know all the lurid details. It was no wonder that that *Yodel* snitch reporter kept showing up for back door dinners and Mardi Gras parties.

He was getting his information straight from the leak himself: Mr. Sewell.

As these Lenten weeks dragged on, I thought a lot about purgatory, that waiting room for the souls of the not-quite-damned. Rose was trapped upstairs in her own drugged limbo, and with no parties to prepare for and no daring, dramatic escapes to orchestrate, my days of maid work became—well, just work. Even the weather was contrary, waffling between wet snow and spitting rain with occasional unkept promises of sunshine.

Every day in the house seemed a drab, pointless exercise, as we all waited to see where we would end up.

"Sisyphean," Alphonse muttered to himself one day as I was sweating and buffing the same spot on the foyer's marble floor where Mr. Sewell's shoes always left a black mark.

I sat back on my heels. "Who's a sissy?" I never let Jimmy Ratchett call me that, and I wasn't about to let Alphonse. Especially as he'd given me the silent treatment for weeks.

Something about this response tickled him, and he stopped and laughed to himself, despite the painting he wrapped his arms around.

"Sisyphus. Although I would not call him a sissy. He was a—how you say?—Strong? No, fierce king, cursed with an impossible task. To roll a large rock up a hill and then watch it roll back down again. The next day he did it again. And the next day. And the next. For eternity."

I looked down. The marble in front of me was spotless, sparkling. For now.

"So it is Sisyphean. Your work and mine. Back and forth, this way and that. But nothing changes." He shifted the weight of the bundle in his arms.

"Coming or going?" I asked, indicating the painting.

"Going." He tipped it down so I could get a peek. It was the painting of Bacchus that Rose had hung for the party.

I nodded. Said nothing.

It was Sisyphean to ask, I thought to myself, because what would be the point? Why endeavor to know anything?

But I did anyway.

"And what's in its place?"

"Nothing."

I stood up. The image of that gallery, empty of Rose's visual schemes, made my heart drop like a stone in a cold, still pond. "Nothing at all?"

He shrugged and twitched his mouth, causing his mustache to dance. It had filled in a bit more, becoming somewhat unruly, and with his high forehead and dark bushy eyebrows, he was beginning to look increasingly like a young walrus.

"No new paintings in the gallery, then?"

Alphonse shook his head. No new messages from Rose. Not only had I destroyed her one chance at escape, I had killed her hope for another.

From several paces away, I craned my neck to peek at Bacchus. "Can I see it? One more time?"

Alphonse glanced around, and seeing no one approaching, set the painting down on the marble floor, leaning against the marble wall. It seemed that marble covered every surface in this house, like a cold white creeping moss.

Now that I had time to stop and really look at the painting, this Bacchus looked funny to me. He may have been a god, but he looked more like Giuseppe, Mr. Latonza's son from the cobbler shop. No long wizened beard or muscled arms that held up the world. This Bacchus was slight and lean, his baby-face cheeks pink with wine, and his toga slipped off in a way that had . . . was it improper to say sex appeal? He held out a thin glass goblet of wine— so shallow it looked like the liquid might spill all over his nice white toga at any moment—but when I looked closer, I saw something strange:

His fingernails were filthy.

Instinctively, I looked at Alphonse. He nodded, as if he'd been waiting for me to get there. "And the fruit," he said.

There, underneath the goblet, was the fruit bowl that seemed to pop up in every canvas, signifying bounty or something like that. There was that gro-tesque pomegranate again, its seedy guts bursting. And around it was fruit of all kinds—some glossy and vibrant, but most . . . bruised, I saw now. Mushy. Rotten.

I stood back. This Bacchus was no god. He was

a half-drunk boy who smirked and beckoned, who pawed food with dirty hands. I would only drink the cup he offered me if I wanted to find myself knocked out and relieved of my pocketbook.

"You see the joke now?"

"Ye-es." I hesitated. "Mr. Sewell?" Alphonse nodded again. "But it doesn't make sense, really. I mean, Mr. Sewell is a teetotaler—"

"Bacchus—how do you say?—he intoxicates. Not only through wine. Through words."

"Through stories." I whispered.

"There is a play by Euripides—you know—?" He stopped himself and smiled, knowing I'd never heard the name in my life. "—A play called *The Bacchae*, in which Bacchus drives his rival mad, then convinces his followers that this man is actually a wild animal. These worshippers, they fall into a frenzy, they tear the man limb from limb with their bare hands—all because of what Bacchus made them believe."

A shiver ran up my spine, not only from the specter of Rose, being carried through the party like wild game fresh from the kill, but from the burst of cold air that had just been let in from the front door.

Mr. Sewell blew in, the door wide open behind him. "Keep it running!" he shouted to the shining black Rolls that had replaced the not-as-new Duesenberg. "By God, isn't someone supposed to be at the door—ah, there you are Alphonse, good," he said, eyes never leaving his pocket watch. He launched in with a barrage of directions involving spilled coffee and his checked shirt and lunch with the mayor, storming past the painting of his alter-ego still leaned against the wall.

By the time he returned in the fresh shirt and tie, I'd returned to my spot on the floor, unfortunately directly in Mr. Sewell's path.

Had it not been for Alphonse's quick hand under the master's arm, Mr. Sewell would have slipped and gone headfirst into the bucket of slop water.

There followed a great deal of swearing and blustering and blinding, as expected, and I bobbed curtsies up and down. But something about the near fall had shaken Sewell out of his focus on shirts and his pocket watch, and as Alphonse helped him regain his footing, the two men found themselves face-to-face.

Maybe it was the mustache, which as I mentioned had become quite luxuriant in the past few weeks. Or maybe Mr. Sewell wasn't accustomed to actually looking at his servants.

But he stopped there for a moment, regarding his footman, the same way Alphonse and I had just been staring intently at the painting.

"Has anyone ever told you—" Sewell started, then narrowed his eyes. "Where did you say you were from?"

Alphonse smiled placidly. "Strasbourg. That eastern part of France that is also Germany, depending who you ask. Perhaps you know it from your travels?" And then he released a stream of French that sounded quite different from Chef's.

Alphonse, I could tell, was gambling that Mr. Sewell didn't speak French, and it was a bet he won. Mr. Sewell looked at the man suspiciously for a moment, then strode away without another word.

But before he left, he turned to me. "Tell your mother I need to speak with her as soon as I return this evening."

I curtsied again, noticing, as I looked down, that Sewell had left another black mark on the floor.

With a groan, I sank back to my knees, while Alphonse turned back to the painting.

"What happened to Bacchus," I asked while kneading the scrubbing brush into the floor, "in the end of that story?"

There was a pause, and when I looked up, I noticed that Alphonse's hands were shaking as he picked up the painting by its frame. "Nothing happened," he said. "He was a god. The gods live forever."

On the way home, I finally understood what had rattled Mr. Sewell so.

It was on one of those long subway rides home, where the silence of the house pursued us all the way to Brooklyn. Ma had started reading the *Standard* with renewed interest, poring over its pages instead of lecturing me about my posture or my work habits. It was as if she was studying for a test, soaking in every word Mr. Sewell had approved with the attention of a scholar.

Like the bearded men on the subway who bobbed and nodded over their prayer books, Ma worked her way backward through the paper, starting with the business section and working right to left up to the headlines.

I tilted my head to read the front page.

ITALIAN BOMB PLOT
FOILED IN CHICAGO

Three men were apprehended today after bomb-making materials were found in the car they were driving and at one of the men's homes. Police suspect the men, two of whom were of Italian origin, of anarchist sympathies and indicated the bombings may have been intended as revenge for the trial and execution of known anarchists and murderers, Sacco and Vanzetti.

My eyes flitted around the subway car, and sure enough, as the other riders opened and folded their *Daily News*, their *Post*s, their *Yodel*s, the same story flashed in and out:

SACCO AND VANZETTI LIVE! SHOUT ANARCHISTS

ANOTHER FOILED PLOT, THANKS TO CHICAGO'S FINEST

With each story, mugshots of three small-fry hoodlums stared out, looking bewildered. But next to them, always, was a photo I'd seen reproduced so many times I'd stopped looking.

It was two men, sitting handcuffed together, side by side, very somber. One was clean-shaven, but the other had a great bushy mustache like a walrus.

Like a thicker version of Alphonse's.

These were Sacco and Vanzetti, the men executed—some said wrongly—a couple of years back. Since then, their supporters had unleashed a string of attempted bombings on those (they said) responsible for their persecution: the judge, a juror, the executioner, the governor. There had even been a bombing at the Twenty-Eighth Street subway station here in New York City, where dozens of subway riders—just like the ones bouncing and dozing their way downtown in this very car—were bloodied.

I peered at the picture of the mustached one, called out as Mr. Bartolomeo Vanzetti. The resemblance was impossible to ignore.

Didn't Alphonse say he had an older brother? A brother who convinced him to immigrate to America? Who, he said, was dead?

I waved away the thought at first. What fish off the boat didn't have a brother along? And a brother who'd died was hardly news. There was no shortage of ways for the poor and hungry to expire in this city.

But most young immigrants didn't share the eyes of America's most hated anarchist, I thought as I stared at the photo that confronted me from every side. Or the same mustache, the same rounded jaw, the same jutting forehead.

Was Alphonse actually Vanzetti's younger brother?

Was it coincidence that he ended up working for Mr. Sewell—the very man whose newspaper had pursued his brother into the electric chair? Who painted his brother as ten kinds of guilty before he even made it to court?

Or was it by design?

Alphonse gave the impression of a defeated

man, and if this story were true, I supposed it made sense. When years of protests, marches, letters, and vigils worldwide couldn't free your brother, why would you believe anything you did would free the wife of one powerful man? A man whose every word became the truth, simply because he owned a newspaper?

But I remembered a story, front page of the tabloids a few years back, about a servant at a fancy club in Chicago. He poisoned the soup at a party, sickening two hundred people. The servant turned out to be an anarchist, and the act his revenge against the rich and powerful.

And I remembered the explosion on Mr. Sewell's very front steps, and Alphonse's mysterious absence.

That's why Alphonse—Alfonso?—Vanzetti, was in that house. Behind that false front of defeated apathy, underneath his cold detachment, he was most likely waiting for the right moment to finish the job.

Ma's eyes met mine over the top of the paper. She saw the picture, too. She saw that I saw. But without saying a word, she folded up her paper, stuffed it in her bag, and closed her eyes, pretending to sleep.

———

The next day, Alphonse had shaved his mustache.

But it was too late.

"May I have a word with you in my sitting room?" Ma beckoned him as soon as she got in that morning.

An hour later, he was gone.

Chapter
25

So then there were four.

Mr. Sewell. Mrs. Sewell. Ma. And me. (Five if you counted McCagg. I didn't.)

And no one was talking.

At least not to me.

Whenever I tried to talk to Ma—to apologize, to ask about Rose, to warn her of the sticky, icky, dark feeling I felt lurking in the silence—she stopped me. "You've done enough. Believe me, you've done enough."

But then everything changed.

One day, in late March, I looked up from my mop and saw that the lion outside had been cloaked in lamb's clothing. Bare trees budded, slush drained into the gutters, and up and down Park Avenue, tulip shoots struggled to break free of their underground exile.

And overnight, the silence of the house had been banished by babble.

Every room in the house now found itself inhabited by a radio, switched on and nattering, one room to the other. It was a bizarre sensation, to say the least. Ma had always hated the radio—"Isn't there enough talking in the world?"—and wouldn't abide them in the servants' quarters, even in the kitchen, where a little music would've helped those dishes wash themselves. But maybe now the silence was getting to her, too.

As I cleaned and polished, chased from room to room with music and news and Pepto-Bismol advertisements, the radios should have been welcome company. But instead it felt like a nervous old biddy trying to fill an awkward break in the conversation. And if I tried to turn it off, Ma swept in behind me and switched it back on. Without a word.

In the midst of that chatter came Rose's last message.

It was a Saturday at the end of March. It was raining—not one of those soft spring rains, but a soaking one, that drenched Mr. Sewell in that short walk from his new Rolls-Royce to the front door. I ran forward to collect his hat and overcoat before the puddle underneath him required a mop.

"Eh—Martha." He looked around and it was as if he'd just noticed I was the only servant left.

"Good evening, Mr. Sewell." The wet coat over my arm had soaked through the left side of my body, but with my dry hand I retrieved an envelope on a side table. "Dr. Westbrook left these papers for you, sir."

If Mr. Sewell could have rubbed his hands together like a movie villain, he would have. Instead his hands were too busy ripping the package open. He scanned the papers quickly, his thin mustache dancing over his twitching mouth.

I strained my eyes to the very corners to peek. I only saw a few words I recognized: *recommendation . . . Rose . . . sanitorium . . . assets transferred.*

My eyes were stopped by Mr. Sewell's own. I lowered them while he stuffed the papers back into the envelope.

"You're a curious girl, aren't you, Martha? So I expect you've been reading the *Standard* then?" He didn't wait for a response. "And what did you think about today's front page? How about that new company we profiled, Ameriwin? Put your money on them, girl; that stock's going to be a skyrocket."

What money, I thought. But I said, "What do they do?"

"Oh, they're on to a very important invention." He tucked the envelope away in his suit pocket. "Trust me."

I didn't. "Well, I do have that extra fourteen cents a week . . ."

This bit of sarcasm flew right over the master's head. "And this is the stock! With the right knowledge," he put his finger alongside his nose, "a chambermaid might become a millionaire, hmmm? As a wise man once said, knowledge is power. Also," he added, glancing at his watch, "time is money."

"Pluck not luck," I murmured in response.

He seemed pleased. "Why yes, exactly! That's what I've been saying. Your destiny is knocking! Seize the reins!" He attacked the metaphors with an eggbeater. "Now when you see your mother, tell her I need to speak to her. In my office."

He patted the envelope in his pocket and hummed his way down the hall.

Before I could summon my mother, I was distracted by a thumping on the stairs.

Thump.

"Ma?"

Thump.

I ran to the bottom of the stairs, expecting to see the end of our little drama unfold: Mr. McCagg drags a heavily sedated Rose down the stairs. Mr. Sewell produces a letter from her doctor, stating that, yes, she would be better off institutionalized. An ambulance appears outside to whisk her away, and all her assets—her house, her paintings—are on the auction block in time for Mr. Sewell to invest the whole lot in Ameriwin. And Ma and I are out of jobs, while Mr. Sewell enjoys penthouse living.

But it was only Ma. In Alphonse's absence, it was her arms wrapped around a painting, almost as big as she was, and it landed heavily as she bumped it down each stair.

"I told her," she huffed to herself—or to me? I wasn't sure. "I told her this was entirely unnecessary. But she never did listen to me."

"Mrs. O'Doyle!" The office door shook with Mr. Sewell's voice. "Is that you? In here, madam, we have much to discuss."

Ma abandoned the painting in the hallway, hurrying to the office where the door closed behind her.

I don't know how I knew. How I knew what it would tell me. Maybe I suspected Rose's desperation. Maybe those few glimpses at Mr. Sewell's documents planted the seeds of dread.

I crept over to the painting, muffling my footsteps from the office or the painting, I wasn't sure which.

No, Rose, I shuddered as I caught the first glimpse. Please, no. Not this plan.

Judith and Her Maidservant read the label, along with a fantastical Italian name I couldn't pronounce, let alone spell.

The painting was simply, dark: two women standing in a dark hall in the dark of night, illuminated only by a beam of light streaming in from a corner. The women are united in their mission and, in the moment, both look nervously over their shoulders, stealing away from that light, as if they're afraid they've been discovered.

The plump one was Judith, I supposed, in her jewels and velvet, the beautiful rich widow who scolds her people for their refusal to fight off an invading army. (I had to offer some silent thanks to Sister Ignatius for grilling us on the Old Testament.) The maid has her back to the viewer, faceless and anonymous, as all maids are. But why so nervous, Judith and Maidservant? Maybe it's your cargo. For Judith has a sword slung over her shoulder like a pirate, while the maid (always left the dirty work) carries a basket containing the blood-dripping head of Holofernes, the enemy leader Judith has just assassinated.

I wrapped my arms around my own shoulders, as if shaking sense into myself. Is this what Rose wanted? My help in destroying—beheading?!?—her enemy?

How? When? Was I the one to plan it? I was a liar, that I knew. I'd even been a thief at times, and certainly a slacker.

But I was not a murderer.

But how else would Rose escape Mr. Sewell's plan to toss her in a loony bin and get his hands on her art, her house, her everything?

And yet, how did trading the loony bin for a spot in the electric chair make for a good plan?

Before I could stop my mind from swirling around these questions, the office door opened. I stayed frozen to the spot before the painting as Mr. Sewell breezed past that ominous prophecy.

"Make up my room, Mrs. O'Doyle," he called over his shoulder as he conquered the stairs, two at a time. "I intend to have a good night's sleep."

The next day was Sunday. Our day off.

My sleep had been fitful, with dreams where swords danced with pomegranates, threatening to split them open with every swing.

All through church, through the boys' stickball game in the rain-slicked streets, through a cold

273

supper and an only slightly warmer bath, I thought only of that sword.

I was the first to wake on Monday morning, the first to dress, and the first out the door, dragging Ma behind me as I raced to the subway.

I had to know what was waiting on the other side of the river.

Chapter
26

Ma, on the other hand, seemed in no hurry. She settled into her seat on the train, paging her way leisurely through the newspaper and finally breaking her silence as we broke through the underground tunnel and burst onto the bridge.

"Do you know what day it is?" she asked as she flipped another page.

I held up a hand to the low-hanging morning sun in my eyes. "Monday. March twenty-fourth. No," I said with a glance at the front page, "the twenty-fifth."

"It's Annunciation Day." She looked at me. "Which is—" she prompted.

This was an easy one. "The day the Angel Gabriel announces to Mary that she'll give birth to Jesus. Aw, no," I whined, "we don't have to go to church for a Holy Day of Obligation, do we?"

"No," Ma said with a twinge of annoyance. "Back home they called it Lady Day, for Our Lady of Sorrows." The sun struck Ma's face with the same brilliance, but she accepted its glare with barely a squint. "Some said it was the day Christ died as well."

"That's Good Friday," I interjected. Surely Ma, practically a saint herself, knew that. "And that's not till, well, Friday."

" 'Tis just a tradition," she continued. "That Christ would be conceived and would die on the same day. That death and birth would twine together. It falls at the vernal equinox, see." She looked out the window, toward the glare. "The first day of spring."

"Some spring," I muttered. Though the sun was out, the wind on the bridge hit so fierce I thought it might blow the car right over.

"Spring isn't marked by fair weather. It's the turn. When the day and the night are the exact same length, and the day starts winning."

But Ma didn't know that the darkest night had already begun to take over Rose's mind. And whatever spring showers or May flowers awaited us would make no difference to Rose—or to me, I thought with dread—in a jail cell.

What shook me out of these frightening thoughts was Ma's hand, her warm, but toughened hand, which I found laid over mine.

"Just remember this," she said quietly. "Christ told us that the world may change in an instant. 'Keep watch,' He said. 'For of that day or hour, know not even the angels in heaven.'"

And as a shrieking wind rattled the train on its tracks, Ma took up her paper again and began to study the business section.

But not in the *Daily Standard*, I noted. Another paper called the *Wall Street Journal*.

Of course, today everyone knows what happened on March 25, 1929.

At least, they think they do.

Afterward, when the events of that night came to light, I was a minor celebrity in the neighborhood. Kids, even adults, stopped me on the street, knowing I'd worked in that house in the previous months.

"What did you see?" they'd ask. "Did you have any inkling?"

I always told the truth—that I had no idea.

Sure, maybe the scale of the destruction wasn't entirely surprising. Like a steam pipe building pressure, at some point it had to blow.

Who could have predicted the death of one of the most important newspaper men of the century, cut down in his prime?

Who could have guessed that this godlike man would let a serpent into his garden? That his killer was under his own roof?

And no one could have dared foreseen the whole-sale annihilation of one of the world's greatest art collections.

The whole thing was impossible to understand. "Unbelievable," folks muttered, shaking their heads over the words, as they followed the grim story over the following weeks.

But, of course, they all did believe it. It was in the papers.

When I arrived that morning, I flew past Ma and abandoned my apron.

"Where are you going?" she shouted after me as I flew up the servant stairs, and then up the front stairs to the family floor, straight to Mr. Sewell's closed bedroom door.

I held my breath. Pressed my ear to the door.
Nothing.
Dragging my courage up from the pit of my stomach, I knocked lightly. Then harder.

Nothing.

The crystal doorknob was surprisingly cold against my palm, but, with my eyes squeezed shut, I turned until I heard it click, then pushed.

Behind my eyelids, my mind conjured the most horrifying scenes I could expect. Mr. Sewell's lifeless, bloody trunk, his head rolled away into the corner? Or—worse?—the master of the house, unclothed and irate?

I opened one eye, then the other. But nothing awaited me over the threshold but a disheveled bed, its covers carelessly tossed aside for a maid to reassemble.

My feet carried me all the way up to the top floor, where Mr. McCagg snoozed fully dressed, his cot pulled across Rose's door. From behind the door, I heard the now-familiar sound of dragging and bumping; Rose was safely inside, sorting through her collection again.

I released a deep breath and headed back down the stairs. It was just another day in the Sewell house.

But as I passed that painting of Judith and her maid and their shared mayhem, still abandoned in the hallway, I knew that behind Rose's closed door, some dark scheme was still in the works.

"And what was that all about?" Ma greeted me in the front parlor with the brass polish and a feather duster.

"I was just checking—Mr. Sewell's not here, right?" I asked with a final glance toward his office. "I mean, he's all right and everything?"

"And what kind of question is that? He's at work, of course, left early as usual." Before I could respond, Ma snapped on the radio in the front parlor. "Now, let's get to business on these front rooms. We have a lot of work to do."

It was somewhere between finishing the piano in the conservatory and starting on the woodwork that I noticed the music had stopped.

So had *Housekeeper's Chat* with Aunt Sammy, and Ruth Turner's *Washing Talks*.

It was just one newscaster after another, no matter the station, following me from room to room, with the same story.

"Nervous investors are dumping stocks by the truckload. . . ."

"A weeklong drop in stock prices has led to a panic down on Wall Street. . . ."

"Stock prices plunge as interest rates skyrocket. . . ."

And I noticed, too, Ma's footsteps quickening throughout the house, up and down the stairs, back and forth across the floors, bringing her finally to my door.

"Quick," she breathed heavily, her face flushed, "run down to the newspaper office and tell Mr. Sewell to get here as fast as he can."

"But can't you—"

"The phone lines are overloaded; I can't get a call through. Quick, Martha! Tell him it's Rose! It's a matter of life and death!"

I couldn't get a cab—it seemed all of the Upper East Side had commandeered them in a caravan to Wall Street—and was afraid the 6 train would be too slow. So I ran all the way down to East Fifty-Third Street.

I worried that I wouldn't be allowed in the *Daily Standard*'s imposing, marble-halled building. But on this day, it seemed even a sweaty, huffing girl in a maid's uniform could go unnoticed. I pushed past reporters who streamed in and out of the bullpen, shouting down phones and clacking on typewriters, until I found Mr. Sewell's office at the very back.

With a tap, I pushed the office door open, and a dozen men—most down to shirtsleeves and coffee stains—stopped dead in their dealings and looked back at me.

Mr. Sewell stood out in the crowd, the only one still with his jacket and tie on, as if taking a stand for decency in the face of Armageddon.

"WHAT," he blasted as soon as he saw me, "could be so *infernally* important that you'd *interrupt*—"

And then he saw, and I saw that his face moved quickly from fury to fear. Fear not for his wife's well-being, but that his well-laid plans were going down at the speed of the market.

Ten minutes later, I sat clammy in the front passenger seat of Mr. Sewell's car, sticking to the fine leather upholstery, as his driver expertly threaded the car around the traffic that clogged Park Avenue. Any fun I might have found in riding in a luxury automobile was dashed with every curse that Mr. Sewell launched from the backseat. And every fleeting observation I made—the car had its own radio right inside!—was tamped back down by a new disturbing image: Rose sick, Rose hurt . . . or worse.

Mr. Sewell flung his door open the moment the Rolls found the curb, and I scrambled out behind him, racing to follow his long stride all the way up to Rose's rooms, where the truth awaited.

But we didn't make it past that newly dusted and gleaming front parlor, where it was hard to say who was more surprised—Mr. Sewell or me—to find a group waiting for us: Ma, Mr. McCagg, Alphonse . . . and Rose.

Chapter
27

Mr. Sewell sputtered his way out of his shock.

"McCagg! This is outrageous! Why is Mrs. Sewell out of her room? For heaven's sakes, man, get her—"

"Uh, sorry, sir." McCagg stared at his feet—coward, I thought—and put his hands protectively on his new employer's chair back. "The missus says I'm not on your payroll anymore."

I couldn't understand what was happening. Why Ma and Rose were sitting calmly on a silk-and-gilded sofa—Rose with her hands folded genteelly on her lap, pale, drawn, but no longer rashy. And why Alphonse and McCagg were standing at attention behind them.

It looked like a bizarre family photo. But it was

actually the very picture of four people in complete control.

And the look of utter panic on Mr. Sewell's face showed that he saw it, too.

"Not on my payr—" He decided to try his luck with Ma. "Mrs. O'Doyle, frankly I'm shocked. What doomed scheme has this riffraff sweet-talked you into." His voice turned from scolding to wheedling. "You know you've always been my best and most trusted teammate. An angel, really, sent from heaven. For Rose and," he ducked his head in imitation of a bashful schoolboy, "and for me."

Ma's composure was steel and stone, as if it were the twins before her swearing no knowledge of the candy wrappers in their schoolbags.

"Come, Martha." Ma ignored Mr. Sewell's little speech and patted a spot on the sofa. "You belong over here."

I willed my feet to take me to the winning team, like a very tense game of Red Rover.

When I sat down, Ma put her hand—that warm, toughened hand—on mine.

Mr. Sewell turned to Alphonse next. I thought it was telling that, while a man his size could easily have commandeered Rose and dragged her back to her rooms, he was powerless without the servants to do his dirty work. I wondered next who would make his bed and rub the black spots out of the floor.

"I suppose this is all your scheme, then. I figured you out, you know—before Mrs. O'Doyle could send you away. You're an *Italian*, correct?" Mr. Sewell spat the words out, as if being born in that country was its own character flaw. "And I'm right that you're related to that Vanzetti somehow, aren't I? Well, out with it. Name your ransom then, and let's get this over with."

Alphonse just gave a little smile, quiet as usual, and turned the stage over to the real star of the show.

Rose.

She cleared her throat, and though her voice was scratchy to start, weak from years of isolation, she was determined to be heard.

"As of this afternoon," she said, her voice thin but growing in strength, "you have nothing with which to threaten McCagg, or me, or any of us. Because with the collapse of the market this morning, I'm guessing your money is gone. And your newspaper is next to go."

Panic crossed Mr. Sewell's eyes although he forced a laugh. "My dear, you really are not well. I've been telling you . . ." And then more seriously: "What would you possibly know about it?"

Rose opened up the scrapbook that I noticed had been sitting on her lap, much like the one I'd found ages ago in the front parlor. But instead of regaling us with tales of her debutante days, she began reading what sounded like excerpts from the *Daily Standard* business section:

"'FED RUMORED TO APPROVE GULF-NORTHERN DEAL'"

She looked up, searching Mr. Sewell's face for a glimmer of recognition. Finding it, she returned to the scrapbook.

"'A SMOKELESS CIGARETTE? SIR WALTER TOBACCO SAYS YES.'"

"'UNITEDCO MANUFACTURING EXPECTED TO ANNOUNCE TECHNOLOGY BREAKTHROUGH'"

"These are just from the last month, although I'm sure there have been hundreds more over the years. The stories are quite the headline grabbers, wouldn't you say?" The small crowd around her all nodded in agreement. "One might even say . . . incredible."

Mr. Sewell looked sick.

"And look here," she flipped to the back of her scrapbook, where (I peeked over Ma's shoulder) another section held clippings from the stock report. "Each of these companies have jumped—indeed, danced to your tune—in the days following your reports. And yet no other newspaper has carried any report of such earth-shattering discoveries. Is the *Daily Standard* really such a beacon of investigative reporting? How *did* you manage all these—'scoops,' I believe they're called?"

I thought of Mr. Sewell's dinners by the cloak of night and those mystery guests: tipsters, shysters, and collaborators.

And *Yodel* reporters being fed incriminating stories about Rose.

"My guess is that you've made money on every front. Payments from the swindlers who got you to plant their questionable 'breakthroughs' on the front page. And, of course, money on the back end, when the stock you'd bought ahead of time suddenly skyrocketed."

As I watched this extraordinary performance, I realized I was finally seeing the *real* Rose—not the sedated Rose, or the panicked Rose, or the rashy, imprisoned Rose. The Rose who had kept her father guessing with her schemes and intrigues and keen business sense. But in the end was only entrusted with fancy paintings, while a nephew got the company and drove it into the ground.

"Well," Rose closed the scrapbook now, "all good things come to an end. But surely you've seen it coming. The signs have been everywhere—the Federal Reserve's warning last week, the Dow-Jones falling steadily. . . . A wise investor like yourself would have moved most of his funds out of the stock market." She smiled at Mr. Sewell's panicked expression. "No? Well then, your portfolio will have been wiped out by," she looked to the grandfather clock in the corner, its hands reaching four o'clock, "right about now."

Mr. Sewell had been stunned into silence all through Rose's speech, but now tried weakly to protest. Rose stopped him with her hand.

"And if not by the end of the day, they will be by the end of the year, when the readers and investors you've duped realize your treachery. By which point you've lost not only your money, but your newspaper's credibility. With one word to the authorities, you'll be out of circulation by Monday. You'll have nothing: not the money your father left you, not the money you conjured in the market, not the machine by which you made it."

Rose let the grim scenario settle over her husband while she folded her hands primly again.

"Unless."

Many years later, a guy at the flea market told me

the secret to negotiating. "Whoever speaks first," he claimed, "loses." I thought of Rose and Mr. Sewell immediately, facing off, with that word—"Unless"—dangling between them.

Mr. Sewell finally cleared his throat, although he tried to disguise it as a guffaw. "Unless what?"

"Unless you accept our generous offer."

"Generous?" he said. "Is that what you call blackmail? My God, I've always known you were—"

"I'd call it generous, seeing as how we've arranged a lovely vacation for you." All the adults nodded together, murmuring at their largesse. "Unless you'd prefer a life of poverty and prison?"

"A vacation?" Mr. Sewell sputtered, looking from face to face around the room, searching for someone who shared his disbelief "That's really—a vacation?"

"Of sorts. There's just one clause in this contract. You have to leave right away." Rose glanced at the clock again. "Right now, in fact."

The absurdity of the situation finally hit Mr. Sewell with full force, and he began to pace and rant around the room, hoping that the full force of his words could push through a loophole.

While the master raged, Ma tut-tutted. "I was at

a performance once," she turned to Rose, "where they gave away a trip to Niagara Falls, so long as you left straightaway from the theater. I must say, the winners were quite delighted with their good fortune, and they weren't even outrunning a national scandal."

Rose shrugged. "Well, you can lead a horse to water . . ."

"Fine. Fine." Mr. Sewell finally paced his way back to the group. "Let's say I go along with this. I'm leaving now, eh? I'll just grab a few things." He turned toward his office.

But Alphonse came around the back of the sofa with a small suitcase.

"We've taken the liberty," Rose interrupted, "of packing a few necessities for you, including some traveling funds. You can buy whatever else you need at your destination." Alphonse handed the case to Mr. Sewell, who looked confused; he'd never carried his own bags before. Alphonse placed the handle in Mr. Sewell's hand and wrapped his master's fingers around it. In Mr. Sewell's other hand, he placed a ticket.

"My destination?" Mr. Sewell looked down at the suitcase in his hand, as if confused by how it got there. "Wait, where am I—"

Rose ignored this as Alphonse left to fetch coats and hats. "Oh, and just one other thing. You'll need to go by the name Alfonso Vanzetti."

"What, on the ship?" His attention shifted to the ticket, and he inspected it, as if it laid out Rose's secret plan.

"Yes. And, well, forever. As of this evening, J. Archer Sewell is no more."

"Now, wait just a—"

"Yes, yes," Rose dismissed his questions with an imperial wave of her hand, "It's all very confusing, I understand. Alphonse will explain it on the way to the docks. And Alphonse, dear,"—he was back, a hand under his master's elbow steering him to the door—"teach Mr. Sewell a few words of Italian, won't you? To help him muddle through the third-class queues?"

And that was the last anyone saw of J. Archer Sewell. By the end of the evening, he was safely installed on the S.S. *Garibaldi*, in a lower-deck cabin shared with five other travelers in bunk beds. In a couple of weeks, he'd be disembarking in Naples, Italy.

Out at sea, he would learn too late that the market's tumble was slowed by some of his wealthy cronies, who propped up the drooping market with vast infusions of cash. But it was a futile effort, and by October twenty-ninth of the same year—Black Tuesday—it was all over. A man like Mr. Sewell, with his net worth strewn all over the market like a roulette wheel, would be wiped out.

But he could begin again, if he liked, in a sleepy Italian seaside village, under the name Alfonso Vanzetti.

But if Mr. Sewell was now Alfonso Vanzetti, who was Alphonse?

"I am already Alphonse Dupont," he told me, handing off a swaddled Rembrandt as part of our makeshift bucket brigade. McCagg, Alphonse, Ma, and I manned various points along the stairs and by the dumbwaiter, as Rose's entire collection of paintings was moved from her room, down the stairs, to the basement hallway, just outside the kitchen.

Each painting was wrapped in whatever sheets, quilts, and fine silk blankets we could pilfer from the Sewell linen closets. I didn't know why. I didn't ask why.

But I stayed close to Alphonse and to Ma, who each exuded calm in the midst of this bewildering afternoon.

"I made this name after my brother's death, to get a job without the prejudice." Alphonse moved past me, tucking what looked to be the Picasso pomegranate under his arm. "It has worked for me so far. So I will continue with it. Mr. Sewell can have my old name."

I handed him another small frame. "Ma—did she know you were . . . Alfonso . . . when she hired you?"

Ma's voice came muffled from behind a large canvas she carried, wrapped in a feather duvet. "I didn't know until you did. With all the photos of Mr. Vanzetti in the paper." She put the bundle down and caught her breath while Alphonse took it over. "It's why I sent Alphonse away. I knew Mr. Sewell would have him turned over to the authorities. And by then, I needed him for," Ma glanced at the hallway operation, "this."

I looked back nervously at Alphonse. "So you are an—an—?"

"An anarchist?" Alphonse looked annoyed, either with me or with the stacked frames that threatened to tumble like dominoes. "Are you a film star because you go to the picture show? Yes, I attended meetings. I attended rallies. I heard different opinions and plans and ideas. I gained knowledge. Knowledge does not change who you are."

"But"—I turned to Alphonse—"the bomb on the front steps . . ."

Alphonse laughed. "That little *scorreggia*? Mr. Sewell make me to patch that together with rubber cement and firecrackers and leave it there. He knew it would attract the attention of the reporters and let him make his little speech."

I sighed with relief. "So you're not really a bomber?"

Alphonse looked at Ma, guiltily, I thought. "Not usually."

"Did you get everything?" Ma asked quietly.

He nodded and tapped a brochure that I noticed poking out of his pocket. *La Salute e in Voi!* read the title.

"Salute Eeee in—" I asked.

"It means, 'health is in you.'"

"What is it, a recipe book?"

"Of a kind."

Before I could pry any further, McCagg appeared with the largest wrapped canvas—from the shape of it, the Judith with the head of Holofernes. He dropped it with the grace of a dockworker. "That's the last one. Where to, Miz O'Doyle?"

Up and down the servants' hallway, blanket-wrapped presents stood ready for their final destination.

But where? Out the trade entrance? While obscured, the entrance was still visible from the street. Anyone walking down the side street would see this operation, and something told me this whole scheme was meant to be secret.

We all turned to Ma for the answer. But she knew as little as we did.

"Let me get Miss Rose. I'd hoped to let her rest more for the journey, but—" She looked up and down the hallway. Everything was ready. "Let me get Miss Rose."

Wearing a patched dress of Ma's, the headline-making, art-hoarding mad heiress was gone.

Standing before of us was simply a shabbier, slightly frailer version of anyone you'd see walking down Willoughby Street. She was no one. She was anyone.

She moved slowly down the hall, economizing her steps, saving her energy for something more important. She dragged her hand over the muffled squares and rectangles like a proud governess seeing her children off to school.

She kept walking—past the servants' entrance, past the kitchen, past the stairs that led to the main floor—all the way to the dark, dead end of the hall, where the doors to Chef's pantry stood closed.

Rose opened them.

Slowly she began to remove the cans, jars, boxes of foodstuff from the shelves inside. Ma nudged me, and we moved forward to take them away, clearing

295

away the pantry into neatly packed boxes we stacked in the kitchen.

Where was Rose going, I wondered, that her journey demanded cans of potted shrimp and caviar?

The shelves finally cleared, Rose turned to McCagg and nodded.

Out came a sledgehammer.

With unmistakable glee, McCagg brought down the full force of his ham arms, splintering the shelves. Then he started in on—good Lord!—the pantry doors and the very walls themselves.

"Ma!" I grabbed my mother's arm, hoping she'd stop him, but she put her arm around my shoulders and passed her sense of calm to me.

The entire wall—up until now nondescript and unnoticed—gave way to McCagg's brute strength, and within minutes, an entirely new escape appeared in the rubble.

Just behind that unremarkable pantry, a portal to another world had lain in wait: a double-high, double door, all oak and mahogany and stained glass, that rivaled the main entrance upstairs. It was the kind of grand entry you'd design for visiting millionaires, the kind who took private train cars from their Hudson Valley country houses directly to your door. The kind of private underground platform you could only have built if you were, say, the head of the Union-Eastern Railroad, like Rose's father, Mr. Pritchard.

That secret entrance had been long abandoned and built over, and as Rose opened the once-glorious doors, we were greeted not by well-heeled guests but by a windstorm of dust and soot, unleashed as a subway train rushed past on a parallel track.

Now I understood why the kitchen rattled every five or six minutes (more during rush hour).

As we all coughed and pushed our way out, we found the platform intact, as were the stairs at its far end. Industrial-looking iron stairs that led up to Seventy-Third Street.

"Proserpina finally escapes Hades," Alphonse smiled. And Ma pushed me gently toward the stairs. "Go ahead. Go and see."

Though the night's air was damp and heavy, it felt fresh in my soot-caked nostrils. I peeked my face out the unlocked street door, surprised to find only an empty, dark sidewalk. The nearby streetlamp must have burned out—or had it been clipped with a well-aimed rock?

I turned back to see the hidden exit behind me, how it blended into the brick and stone, in an anonymous line of trade entrances and fire doors. How many times had I walked past that drab gray facade and unremarkable sign: CAUTION: DO NOT BLOCK?

I turned back to look up and down the street, shivering from the night's chill. And from the unsettling presence of a hearse, parked right by the exit.

I looked closer.

The driver's window rolled down slowly.

I saw, with a smile, that Ma had found the only driver in town who brought his own dancing skeletons, who uncomplainingly shared the passenger's seat.

Daddo.

"I heard you need a getaway driver," he said with a sadness that served as an apology. "Sorry I'm late."

As the bucket brigade reformed, ferrying paintings from the hallway to the platform and up the stairs to the hearse, I saw now where Rose had been heading that night last fall when she fell out of the dumbwaiter (starting that headline-making fire when she accidentally brushed an olive-oil soaked rag into a pilot light). By making her way to the kitchen, she'd hoped to somehow break into the pantry and onto the platform, escaping by that unnoticed street door.

She'd landed in that *Daily Yodel* reporter's note-pad instead.

The notepad.

I snuck back inside to Ma's sitting room, where'd I'd caught the *Yodel* reporter the night of the party, calling in his report.

And there behind the drapes in the corner, right where I'd kicked it, was his notepad.

"Property of Silas Fowler," it read.

The operator gave me the number for the *Daily Yodel* newsroom, which, as I expected, was open even at this time of night. A young cub said he'd track down Silas for me when I said I had the scoop of a lifetime.

"Who is this?" Silas shouted over the static. "Whaddaya want?"

"Never mind who this is," I answered with a calm that would have made Rose proud. "Just come to the Sewell mansion at—let's say two a.m.—if you want the scoop of a lifetime. And tell your boss to stop the presses."

It was almost one a.m. by the time we had the hearse packed up. It had been an ingenious choice, I thought at the time. Roomy enough in the back to fit the paintings stacked one on top of the other, but practically invisible to meddling outsiders. Who's going to pull over a hearse for inspection?

"It's time to go, Martha," Ma was saying. "Say good-bye."

I started with Alphonse who was eager to get upstairs. He had "work to do," Ma said, and by the presence of Creak and Eek under his arms, I understood it now. He'd leave the skeletons upstairs when he set off the bomb. That would make people believe both Mr. and Mrs. Sewell had perished in the blast.

Alphonse shook my hand, one colleague bidding good-bye to another.

"Where will you go?" I asked.

"Who knows?" he shrugged, but with more a sense of adventure than apathy. "This is the land of opportunity, yes? I can travel light. My only valuables are skills, knowledge, experience. With these, you can go anywhere."

"That's awfully optimistic of you, Alphonse."

He laughed and stroked that bare space where his mustache used to be. "Yes, well, I would say I have more—how did you say?—optimism these days. It is a new beginning." He pulled my ear. "For you too, Martha. Do not forget it."

And dragging Creak and Eek behind him, he

headed off to set the explosion, like the anarchist he never expected to be.

"Say good-bye, Martha."

McCagg had already run off, his silence bought with the Sewell family silver, on his way to the pawnshops of Woodside and then the Belmont racetrack.

I hugged Daddo, my arms squeezing the breath out of his ribs in both love and leftover resentment. I extracted promises to write, to visit, to stop drinking, to find a new agent. His breath was warm and smelled of peppermints—only peppermints—as he swore to walk the straight and narrow, and I knew, in his sober state, he'd make it at least as far as Brooklyn.

That was all Rose needed today. The three of us—Daddo, Ma, and me—helped Rose to the passenger side. Ma settled her in and tucked a small suitcase under her feet. As Daddo took his place behind the wheel, Ma held tight to Rose. They whispered in each others' ears, wiping their tears on each others' hair. A warm spring wind carried the smell of green off the park, and I understood why Proserpina's mother, Ceres, gave the earth back its life just to free her daughter.

Ma pulled herself away.

I still stood holding the door, looking down on Rose.

She looked stronger now. Her hair seemed thicker, flax instead of straw, in its neat but unfashionable bun. Her cheeks were thin but flushed, her eyes no longer sunken but sparkling with excitement. I wasn't worried she might collapse in drugged fatigue or bolt like a nervous pony. And yet, she looked anonymous. The closer she came to her former glory, the more her exterior lied, told a story ordinary and unremarkable. I think Rose preferred it that way.

"You did it."

"No, it was you." She grabbed for my hand. Her hand was warm now, like Ma's.

"I—I didn't do anything. Anything I did only made things—" I glanced toward the back of the hearse. "I just mean—you and Ma made *this* happen. And Alphonse. And Daddo. I just—"

"You believed me. That was enough. That was what started it all." She placed her cheek on my hand. "You believed me."

I believed her.

"Say good-bye, Martha," prompted Ma one more time.

I took back my hand, still wet with Rose's tears,

and gently closed her door. As soon as I stepped back onto the sidewalk, Daddo turned on the engine and slowly pulled the hearse away from the curb, taking Rose, her gallery, and him away.

I never saw any of them again.

Thanks to the call I'd made to the *Daily Yodel*, the next day the story Rose had orchestrated ran on the front page, as follows:

BOMB KILLS NEWSPAPER TYCOON AND HIS "WILD ROSE"!

Priceless Art Collection Destroyed!

Rose "battier than a church bell!" says maid.

Chapter
28
May 2016

In the passing years, I've made up many stories of my own.

Some are about Daddo, of the acts he's created under different names. He had this amazing talent of balancing anything on his face—chairs, bicycles, you name it—and now, wouldn't that have made a great act? But as I'd flip around the channels on the radio and then the television, I knew there was no place for Daddo anymore.

Some stories are about Willy and Timmy, about what they would have done with their lives, had they not given them up on beaches in Normandy and Okinawa. I like to imagine Willy pitching for the Yankees and Timmy for the Mets—or more likely, running a joint plumbing business and spending their nights at Dom Donovan's.

I loved to picture Mr. Sewell, wasting away in an Italian seaside village where "right now" means "sometime next week" and the top headlines include the bocce results. It would be his very own Sisyphean hell to watch the days wash in and out with no more consequence than the tide. And surrounded by all those Cath-o-licks? I've smiled every single time I've thought of it.

But most of my stories are about Rose. Whenever I picked up the paper, I'd scan it for daring women of a certain age. Was this Effie Edelstein, widow and Bronx real estate mogul, Rose reincarnated? Is this Rose, this Baroness Livia Stroganov, the mysterious Russian emigree who founded a cosmetics empire? Or a certain Josie Ann Jenkins, who flew stunt planes, led safaris, and married seven times?

Other days I found myself resentful that I was reduced to these wonderings and wanderings. Why didn't Rose "kill off" Mr. Sewell and save herself? Expose him and claim her rightful place—in her house, with her books, furniture, paintings?

But they weren't hers, those things. They were her father's, or Mr. Sewell's, or some other man's. I think she relished starting over on her own terms, perhaps even in the life of a Jane Smith in Nowheresville, PA: trips to the grocery, haggling over the electric bill, a little TV at the end of the day.

Maybe she wanted to rewrite her history, as the hero—no matter how mundane—of her own story.

This thought stayed with me through the years. When I forced myself to pay attention in class, through nursing school, to stay awake on my feet through the late shift—only to take orders from doctors with half my experience and twenty percent of my brains.

No. I would be the hero of my own life. I would write the story.

It's why I gave up nursing to study pharmacy. Like my friend Dr. Murphy, so many years ago.

It's why I opened my own drugstore, where people came to me with their problems instead of the other way around.

It's why I never married.

For years, Ma and I hunkered down in that house on Willoughby Street, stacking locks and deadbolts on the doors, watching the pubs and shops around us become liquor stores with bulletproof windows. Ma died a month after Nixon resigned. It was breast cancer, but she fought it—right there at home—until her dying breath.

I carried on alone behind those locks until one spring day around the turn of the new century. I noticed a new place where Joe's Shoe Repair had been, before Joe moved to his daughter's on Long Island. It was a coffee shop—well, what we would have called a coffee shop, but what the youngsters called a café, with everyone sitting over a computer and cups of coffee that cost more than the early-bird special at the diner. Another one came, and then a shop that sold bicycles, and then another that sold the same vinyl records that I had put out on the curb when my hi-fi gave out.

Not long after that, I sold Ma's house for one million dollars to a young family wearing dungarees.

So now I was a millionaire. Like Rose.

I bought myself this place at Shaded Acres, right across from once-fancy Green-Wood Cemetery and the Pritchard crypt on the hill. Looking this evening, as the sun begins to set, I can see the roses just starting their last song of the season.

Meet me here, they call, where Rose is laid to rest.

Well, not Rose. Mrs. Eek, actually.

If these flutters in my heart are telling me something, I'll be reunited with Mrs. Eek soon. Rose prepared a place for me in that crypt, back in 1929. In those scheming weeks before she fled, she had Ma

307

drop an update to her will in the mail. There was nothing notable about the change. It was so minor it didn't even occur to the lawyer to alert Mr. Sewell. It read simply:

In gratitude for their loyal service, I extend to Mary O'Doyle and her offspring the invitation to be buried alongside me in the Pritchard plot, should they wish it.

Ma did not wish it. The world wasn't ready to open that crypt, to see what Rose laid to rest, she said. Just look at it—heroes being assassinated, presidents lying, people throwing garbage on the streets. The world doesn't deserve beauty; they'll only destroy it, she said.

But the way I see it is—hasn't it been long enough?

Hasn't the world always been full of monsters and lies? Isn't it our place to fight them, to tell the truth, to rewrite the story? To ensure the return of spring in a world of winter?

Anyway. I've told my story. Now it's time to let the paintings tell theirs.

When I die, I'll be brought to that plot I've watched over all these years. The doors will be opened, and the paintings that Daddo delivered the night of Rose's funeral—unnoticed, unloaded from the back of that hearse—will be resurrected.

The paintings that once told Rose's story will now tell their own.

They'll tell the story of Proserpina and Judith and Sophonisba and even Bacchus. Their own myths. Their stories that have remained the same through centuries, yet been reborn with every new telling.

And they'll tell them again one day. One day, very very soon.

Author's Note

If you're ever bored, go online and search a random year and a topic that interests you—say, "heiresses" or "bombings" or "poison." You'll find yourself trawling old newspapers from around the world, with stories like this:

August 1, 1920:

> For a week the people of Florence have been in a state of intense excitement over the mystery of Miss Anna Wright, a young American heiress, said to be worth $60,000,000, who was said to be kept prisoner in an upper apartment of the palatial Villa Bragiotti, on the plea of being afflicted with precocious madness. . . .

September 27, 1932:

The home of Judge Webster Thayer, 74-year-old jurist who sat during the Sacco-Vanzetti trial, was destroyed early today by a dynamite bomb that injured his wife and a maid. . . .

June 22, 1919:

Heiress bride poison victim; husband taken; wife says mate gave her powders, then left her. In the case is a tangled tale of a jilted suitor, gold mines, property, and a short and speedy courtship. . . .

February 12, 1916:

The police are searching for Jean Crones, assistant chef of the University Club, because of a virulent poison which was found by chemists in soup which was served at the banquet in honor of Archbishop Mundelein Thursday night. A search of Crones's room revealed a quantity of a similar poison and anarchist literature. . . .

How could any fiction writer top this? I certainly couldn't; my only solution was to steal all the best bits and mash them up together.

The result is *The Gallery*.

Newspapers were just the beginning. My research took me through heiresses' biographies, maids' memoirs, society pages, police reports, floor plans, vaudeville lineups, Ellis Island, not to mention real-life museums and mansions.

Along the way, I was continuously surprised by how the realities of history were not exactly what I'd absorbed in school. (For example, did you know it's a myth that your great-grandfather/grandmother's name was "changed at Ellis Island"? No new documents were created at the great Registry Room; the name change would have occurred at the beginning of the journey, on the ship's manifest, or passenger list.)

I'm sure the reader will be surprised, too. Read on to discover what was history, what was fiction, and where one inspired the other.

Are the paintings in the book real?

Yes! Every one. I had fun "shopping" the world's

greatest museums, building my own collection of paintings, and then arranging them to tell Rose's story.

The Gallery's stars, in order of appearance:

Proserpina, Dante Gabriel Rossetti (1874)—THE TATE MUSEUM, LONDON

Still Life with Apples and a Pomegranate, Gustave Courbet (1872)—THE NATIONAL GALLERY, LONDON

Still Life with Ewer, Vessels, and Pomegranate, Willem Kalf (1646)—THE GETTY MUSEUM, LOS ANGELES

The Pomegranate, Pablo Picasso (1912)—THE FOGG MUSEUM, CAMBRIDGE, MA

Sophonisba,* Rembrandt van Rijn (1634)—THE PRADO, MADRID

Pierrot and Harlequin, Pablo Picasso (1920)— BALTIMORE MUSEUM OF ART

Bacchus, Caravaggio (1595)—THE UFFIZI, FLORENCE

Judith and Her Maidservant, Artemisia Gentileschi (1614)—PALAZZO PITTI, FLORENCE

*The subject of this Rembrandt painting is the source of debate: classical heroine Sophonisba or ancient Greek queen Artemisia? Because Sophonisba's story was a better fit to mine, I chose this interpretation.

Gilded Age mansions didn't have their own underground train platforms, did they?

Mansions may not have, but a very famous hotel does. When the Waldorf-Astoria was built, just such a platform was added to give high-profile celebrities a discreet way in and out of the hotel. It was used most frequently and famously by wheelchair-bound Franklin Delano Roosevelt. (FDR's administration worked hard to hide the president's disability from photographers.)

The hotel platform still exists today, but has fallen into disrepair and is no longer in use.

1928–1929: Prohibition, the presidential election between Herbert Hoover and Al Smith, the murder of Al Rothstein, the run on the stock market. Did these things all really happen that year?

They sure did. I was particularly interested in the way the Smith–Hoover election mirrored themes in our own political landscape.

But the stock market crash of 1929 didn't happen until October! Why does the book have it taking place in March?

It was a different crash—a "run-up" crash, economists call it. After the Federal Reserve warned of rampant stock speculation, interest rates started to rise. Investors got nervous and started dumping their stock. Things snowballed the week of March 18, with a market experiencing a mini-crash on Monday, March 25—the day Rose gets the drop on Mr. Sewell.

From reading her husband's newspaper, Rose could tell he was pumping certain stocks for his own gain and was likely overextended in the market. She knew a crash would wipe him out—and she guessed one was coming eventually. So when she heard the radio reports on March 25, she knew he was—at least momentarily—penniless. Just the time to put her plan in motion.

Rose is smart to get Mr. Sewell out of the country that very day. He's already at sea when some of his banker cronies bail out the market, artificially buoying it for another few months—before the Great Crash of October 29.

But how can Mr. Sewell just jump on a ship bound for Italy, with no passport, no visa, just a ticket in Alfonso Vanzetti's name? Wouldn't he have to show identification?

Nope. All of the documentation we take for granted these days—passports, visas, photographic drivers' licenses—didn't exist at this time. At least, not to leave the country.

For some, visas were required to *enter* the country—especially for those immigrants from less "desirable" regions specified in the Immigration Restriction Act of 1921. (Alfonso and his brother would have entered the country before that.) But passports and travel visas didn't become standard until World War II.

Not surprisingly, it was quite easy for people to change their identities at this time—as we see in Alfonso Vanzetti's use of the name Alphonse Dupont.

How could Alfonso get a job under a false name, Alphonse Dupont? Wouldn't somebody check his Social Security number or something?

Again: no. Social Security numbers and other forms of identity documentation didn't come about until the 1940s. At this time, most employees (and certainly servants) were paid in cash or by check, with no payroll taxes extracted. The most a job candidate needed to produce was a reference, which could be easily faked.

Did Vanzetti really have a brother?

If he did, it wasn't Alfonso (or Alphonse). The character of Alphonse is purely fictional, although

Sacco and Vanzetti were very real and very important figures of this time.

Who were Sacco and Vanzetti anyway?

Sacco and Vanzetti were two Italian immigrants who were tried and executed for shooting a security guard as part of a failed robbery.

But the case was a little more complicated than that.

Throughout the 1920s, the political movement known as anarchism was under deep suspicion—partly due to its commitment to change through violence, partly for its large following among immigrants, mostly Italians. Italian anarchists were the face of "terrorists" at this time; they were behind a number of high profile attacks: the bombing on Wall Street in 1920, an attack on a New York City subway train in 1927, the large-scale poisoning mentioned in the headlines earlier. Bombs were their preferred mode of attack: their leader, Luigi Galleani, published a pamphlet misleadingly titled *La Salute é in Voi!* (*Health Is in You!*), which detailed how anyone could build weapons of destruction from everyday items. (It's what appears in Alfonso's pocket the day the Sewell mansion burns to the ground.)

Sacco and Vanzetti had attended anarchist meetings, although their participation seems to have been minimal. They were not even necessarily at the location of the robbery in question. But their anarchist leanings made great headlines in the newspapers of magnates like William Randolph Hearst (a model for Mr. Sewell). Today most believe that Sacco and Vanzetti were scapegoated for their political beliefs, and even at the time their case caused public outcry around the world.

After Sacco's and Vanzetti's executions, a slew of revenge bombings followed, including a failed assassination attempt on Herbert Hoover in Argentina. As the publisher of a paper that had vilified the two men, Mr. Sewell would likely be concerned about revenge attacks as well. (And as it turns out, he even fakes one as a publicity stunt on the eve of the presidential election.)

Were you inspired by any real-life museums or collectors?

Oh, yes. In fact, *The Gallery* has its roots in one of my favorite places, the Isabella Stewart Gardner Museum in Boston. Isabella, very much a model for Rose, was your textbook eccentric Gilded Age heiress with the money and moxie to do as she pleased—

whether it was walking lion cubs on a leash, wearing a Red Sox headband to the opera, or curating a world-class art museum in her home.

Isabella left behind an airtight will leaving her home as a museum. She stipulated that if a single object were ever moved from where she'd placed it, the entire collection should be sold off and the museum shut down. For this reason, when you visit the museum, you will see it exactly as Isabella intended.

Or almost. In 1990, gunmen raided the museum and stole thirteen works of art—including works by Vermeer, Rembrandt, Manet, and Degas. Thankfully the removal of these pieces didn't necessitate the liquidation of the museum. (Isabella's will provided a loophole for theft, cleaning, or lending.) But it did leave the collection diminished, and the museum has left the empty frames in their places as a reminder of what was lost.

(A free-willed heiress. A precise order of paintings. An elaborate heist. I told you I stole my best ideas from history.)

In recent years, leads around the Gardner theft have begun bubbling up to the surface, but there have been no grand revelations yet. I like to think of the paintings waiting somewhere, like Rose's at the end of *The Gallery*. Are they stacked in the dark of a basement, or are they lighting up a living room for an audience of one? Maybe, like Rose's, they're in a cold, sealed tomb in some unsuspecting graveyard. Wherever they are, they're ready to be discovered and to tell their stories again.

Who knows who will find them? Maybe even you.

LAURA·MARX·FITZGERALD studied Art History at Harvard and Cambridge Universities. Her first book for children, *Under the Egg,* was the winner of the New Atlantic Independent Booksellers Association Best Middle Grade Book of the Year award. Laura lives in Montclair, New Jersey.

Learn more at
www.lauramarxfitzgerald.com
and follow Laura on Twitter
@marxfitzy.